What to Suspect When You're Suspecting

Book 2 of The Gus Chronicles

by Karryn Nagel

PROMISE PRESS

Dedication

This book is dedicated to all the ones who survived oppression long enough to tell their stories, and to those who speak about the history of the marginalized and oppressed peoples. It is my sincerest wish that we all may learn and do better by being inclusive with every future generation.

Content Warnings

(** items are referenced, but not explored in detail)

- Transgender ftm topics such as misgendering, Latin family dynamics
- Animal rights
- Military presence
- Large crowds/general public/group behavior
- Political conflict
- Pressure, anxiety
- Profanity

**Death
**Experimentation
**Foster care
**Gender discrimination
**Hate crimes
**Homophobia
**Military force

CHAPTER 1

Mid-March

Nico breathed deeply as he entered the toasty-warm kitchen, enjoying the faintest tang of Brant's latest delectable, cranberry and orange scones, scattered across the kitchen island on cooling racks. They mirrored the toys chaotically thrown across the living room floor. Ignoring the messy view into the other room, Nico perched himself on a bar stool facing the window, savoring the barest hint of Brant's secret ingredient, thyme, as it teased his taste buds to life. He watched the early spring sunbeams through the kitchen window as they struggled to pierce the northwestern clouds streaming across the backyard. It was early, barely half past six in the morning, and he was exhausted. Parenting a dragon was, as the kids say, no effing joke.

Brant was still dead asleep; the sounds of his snores could be heard faintly under the master bedroom door. The long days at the new food truck lot were taking so much out of him, and between that and parenting Gustopher, Nico didn't have the heart to wake him, even though Nico knew he should be up by now.

Nico crept over on tiptoes towards Brant's door, the scone perched on a napkin in his hand. He ever so gently turned the handle, knowing what he would see and needing to see it anyway. The early mornings of their motley family were always the best.

Through the open few inches of the cracked door, Nico could see Brant sprawled across his bed on his stomach, one arm raised above him as if he were hailing a taxicab. His legs were also in a running motion, one knee raised up while the other was curved back. And lying right on Brant's back, sprawled mid-flop, little grey-green ears curved back, three clawed feet dangling down, chin resting on his dad with a satisfied smile at the corners of his mouth, was Gustopher the dragon.

Nico smiled involuntarily at the view. It had been a wild six months of adjustment since that fateful, crazed 72 hours of last September when Nico and Brant had met Gus, Remi, Jasper, and the hockey boys. Nico never could have predicted what he was getting into. Had he known at the time, would he have chosen differently? He considered the idea briefly. While Nico knew he was cautious about making decisions, he was not one to regret his choices. Transgender people faced such scrutiny, invasion of privacy, and constant judgment that there was no room to second-guess. Once you had a decision in hand, you had to stick with it because you would certainly be challenged about it regularly. Of course, not all trans people were like him. Most of them were much braver: going to demonstrations and protests, fighting hateful proposed legislation, and working hard on keeping inclusivity in educational materials at primary schools. Nico wasn't ready to start living so loudly about the trans aspect of his life, but he appreciated the efforts of the queer community deeply.

Nico stepped into the room, keeping as silent as possible as he made his way over to the bedframe. He leaned down and gently placed the barest kiss against the top of Gus's head. Gus didn't stir, just continued wearing his secret smile and sighed contentedly. Gus hadn't grown very much in the last 6 months, only a few inches on all sides. Now he was a little bigger than a Boston terrier.

Nico walked around the other side of the bed and carefully pulled up on the covers that had been kicked aside, laying them gently over Brant's back and shoulders to keep the spring chill from waking him. He exited the room as silently as he had come in, and headed for the bathroom, brushing the last of the scone's crumbs from his bathrobe as he shut the door quietly to begin getting ready for work.

Thirty minutes later from the comfort of his SUV, Nico was still marveling over the changes that had occurred as he drove to the Japanese botanical gardens where he worked as an exhibit bodyguard. The 'bonsai bodyguard,' he had joked originally when he met Brant. The bonsai exhibit was still a major tourist attraction in Multnomah's botanical gardens, so it made sense that he was viewed that way. He even viewed himself that way. But it wasn't all that he did. Nico's responsibilities had grown even more in the last six months, as he had been consulted by management several times on expanding their kids' outreach program. Nico had a knack for helping to keep the crowds moving on the garden grounds when it came to large parties.

Shortly after the showdown with Rubra, Nico had moved in with Brant so they could raise Gus jointly. It had been a hectic scramble to try to develop a routine that worked for their schedules now that Remi had disappeared, and the hockey boys had finished their vacation and headed back to their original destinations. Brant had completed the build-out on his food truck, Bohunkus, and was fully licensed and operational, but this meant he had left his night job bodyguarding and was now working during the day just like Nico. The original overlap of having two parents with different work shifts had been somewhat easier before. Thankfully, they had help from two sources now as both Paula and Koffe could help out at least a few times a week.

Paula had defected from Rubra's employment when she met Gustopher and had been helping out steadily when it came to dragon-sitting. Nico and Brant had originally met Koffe when they went to the Golden Knight dance club, and he had thrown them all out when Remi almost snapped a guy's neck trying to protect Gus. Nico didn't like to dwell on that memory too much.

Koffe had ended up running into Brant in the month after that on the nightclub circuit they both worked, and they had struck up a friendship. Koffe offered to help Brant finish the build-out on the cookie truck, and Gus loved having the big bouncer around. Gustopher would climb on his back, curl around his neck, and generally made the mammoth man laugh when Gus handed him the tools he needed to finish installing a counter, a wallboard, or some flooring.

Without Paula and Koffe, Nico didn't know how he and Brant would've survived. The house was regularly in a maelstrom of dirty dishes, shredded toys, and clothes strewn about. The long, quiet nights of sleep were a distant memory that he longed for, the way a city dweller longs for the crisp, fresh air of the mountains. He barely had time to eat a piece of fruit or grab some cold rotisserie chicken between chasing Gus or trying to clean, cook, or sleep. Working out every other day seemed like a dreamy wish, and he missed the straightforward joy of sweat and simple reps more than he ever thought he would.

Gus had been getting a little bit bigger as the weeks went by but was more prone to the same growth spurts a human toddler went through. Nico recorded what progress he could in his notebook, but there often wasn't time to get his observations in writing. Gus's appetite had grown along with him, and the first few weeks were very stressful as Nico and Brant tried to keep Gus on the live-bird-only diet they had started in the fall. The pet store owners were baffled by the orders they were placing as they evaded describing exactly what they were trying to feed. Eventually, they realized that supplementing the live birds was the only way forward and started to incorporate insect meal every day. It was high in protein, easy to order and store, and came in a variety of flavors. This was a game-changer and took a great deal of pressure off Gus's dads in those early days. Gus had stopped trying to play games of hide n' seek when it was mealtime out of protest with the supplemental food.

Along with Gus's growth had come more of his attitude, especially when it came to communicating. Gus was very impatient with telling his dads what he needed or wanted, whether it was food, attention, games, or affection. Desperate one day, Nico had been buying some more birds from the pet store when his bleary eyes spotted the communication buttons mat for dogs and cats prominently on display. On impulse, he bought the mat and brought it home. Brant was grouchy that he hadn't even researched the success rate or looked up any reviews, but both of them were delighted and surprised when Gus took to it on the first day. If anything, the mat was almost too effective, as Gus started putting together more and more word fragments by the week.

Those first few months had truly been a bit of a scramble, but with the right cocktail of food, communication, and outside help, now Brant and Nico could almost resemble real adults when out in public. They even had time to shower. On occasion.

Nico felt proud looking back at all they had accomplished over the winter. He pulled into the parking lot of the botanical garden and turned the car off. As the sun warmed him through the window, he noticed he had some time until he had to clock in. He pulled out his growth tracker notebook to spend a few minutes cataloging the recent changes in Gus's attitude, behavior, diet, and vocabulary.

Chapter 2

As Nico was heading home later that afternoon, he turned on the radio just as one of the DJ's announced in a near-mania of glee, "And you won't want to miss our next guest coming on after the commercial break! He's a guest lecturer at Osten University, here to break down the social significance of having a baby dragon among us in Multnomah! Stick around to hear this EXCLUSIVE interview with a man who has traveled the world, gathering stories on dragon mythology for 40 years! Just because he wears a winged coat and winged shoes doesn't mean he isn't on to something!"

The DJ cued a laugh track and Nico visibly winced at how the DJ was trying to provoke the radio audience. The DJ was giving the listeners a sense that they were about to hear some never-before-heard point-of-view about Gus. Local news stations had been amping up the public for the last month as word of Gustopher had spread. The DJ continued, "And then at the top of the hour, we will also be hearing from a representative of Mayor Flint's office!"

While he and Brant had initially worked to keep Gus relatively under wraps from the human population, there was never a chance that Gus would be a secret forever. When Nico had first met Gus, he had thought he was a gargoyle. It was an easy mistake to make, as gargoyles shared many features with dragons of myth and legend: long or pointed ears, sharp teeth, often four-legged, with wings and talons. The defining difference was that gargoyles were stone figures that guarded estates and churches and dragons were real — as it turns out — and could breathe fire and let out strange sound waves. Other than that, Nico still hadn't found out much about Gus in particular. He knew he could be studying up on dragons from classical texts and tales, but he was, frankly, too tired.

The magical community had dismissed the news of Gus as a hoax and decided that the rumors about Gus being a dragon were unfounded and human hysteria. Brant and Nico had both been relieved, as they had worried that some faction of the magical community might come forward to either take Gus or imprison him.

Brant had expressed concern about what the public would do when they did find out about Gus, but like Nico, was too exhausted to come up with a definitive plan. It's not as if they could hide; too many people knew at this point. It's not as if they could run; global technology allowed for near-instant communication across continents; they would be immediately identified unless they went to live in underground caves. Nico immediately thought of plants he could grow without much sunlight and dismissed the idea as silly. This is what happens when you have a perpetually tired parent brain. One minute you are listening to the radio and the next you are wondering if you can survive with your co-parent and baby dragon in an underground cave system and worrying about the state of your imaginary houseplants.

It was overcast but warm as Nico pulled into the driveway at home. The clouds of the Pacific Northwest were always rich with texture and dimension, and today was no exception. It often looked as if you were under six layers of feather blankets, only the blankets were the entire sky. Nico was so busy admiring the skyline that it wasn't until he was stepping out of the car that he noticed a small gathering on the sidewalk across from the house. They had camp chairs, coolers, and signs scrawled illegibly that he couldn't make out. He stood still, trying to assess the situation the way Brant had taught him. Today, Brant was at the food truck lot and Gus was being watched this afternoon by Koffe. So, it was up to Nico to determine if there was a threat. It's possible they were there for some other neighborhood event, but he didn't recall hearing about anything in the local newsletter.

His stomach lurched at the scene before him. It might be the Gus enthusiasts, the Dragon Hunters, as they called themselves. Ever since the media had heard the news, they had been encouraging their listeners to "track down" the dragon, and some of Multnomah had taken this seriously. Since both he and Brant were seen in the casino last fall, descriptions of them had been circulating for weeks. Brant had had an easier time, as he ran his own business, but Nico had been approached a few times in the gardens, and he would make an excuse and hurry away. He had hoped the public wouldn't find out where they lived for a bit longer, but it looked as if this was the day all that changed.

Nico could see the gathering of about four or five people. They seemed relaxed and were conversing easily. He didn't recognize any of them, so they couldn't be his fellow neighbors. The neighbors had only seen Gus a few times in passing, and they were still under the impression that he was a gargoyle. They had all taken the attitude of live and let live, and he and Brant were deeply grateful for it. Today, however, he decided to bite the bullet and find out what information the group had and what their intentions were.

As he approached, the group chattered excitedly amongst themselves. A few rose out of their chairs in greeting. Nico picked an older, very petite woman in the group. She looked as if she had just finished knitting a cap for a grandkid and came to watch a tulip contest. And yet despite her demure appearance, she was the one they all gravitated toward.

"Hello. I'm Nico. What brings you all to the neighborhood?" Nico opened in his friendliest fake voice, the one he used for people he had to chastise at the gardens but still wanted them to have a good experience.

"Hello there! We are hoping to get a glimpse of the little fella we all heard about on the radio. Are you one of his guardians?" The older woman inquired with enthusiasm; her penciled eyebrows raised in anticipation. Nico glanced around and saw the same eagerness on their faces. His heart sank. Somehow, his address had been leaked, and the gawkers had come to stare and gossip about Gus. It was the worst possible reason. Nico wasn't amazing under pressure and wasn't sure if he could lie convincingly on the spot. *No time like the present*, he thought.

"Little fella?" Nico replied, repeating it back with a note of forced confusion. He winced internally. It didn't sound convincing, but he kept going. "Not sure who you are talking about or why you would think he'd be here." He decided to try throwing them off the scent. "If you are talking about that little dragon, I heard he lives out by the hospital. Something about a big stone house, with towers and everything. Huge lawn. Carriage house. The works." Nico found himself describing a property he drove by every day on his way to work. The faces looking back at him grew hesitant, and the older woman looked disappointed briefly. She had a shrewd expression though, and she frowned at Nico. He quailed slightly at her look and tried to fix his face with a look of confusion. Brant would scold him later; he was sure of it.

"That's strange. I thought for sure we had found out where he lived." She carried on, "I just wanted a glimpse and maybe a picture or two, you know, for my grandson. He's just wild about dinosaurs and all kinds of ancient and exotic creatures," she said, oblivious to the wry smile that had crept onto Nico's face. "There was a radio contest, you see, and several of us put together the clues after talking it over on one of those, what do you call it? a chat parlor? Only it's on the computer?" She said, marveling at the technology. Someone from the back could be heard muttering "Chat forum, you goose." The other people were looking uncertain at Nico's response. Maybe he had managed to convince them of his lie after all.

Nico could make out one of their signs now that he was up close. It was poorly written, but one was scrawled in red with the words, "WE ARE READY, TEACH US" which was unsettlingly vague on its own. Did they think Gus was some sort of savior? Nico snorted under his breath. *If only they knew the tantrums he threw, they wouldn't think so highly of him then.*

"Well, I gotta get started on dinner. Good luck to you all." Nico said, dodging the subject and looking down, waving a hand goodbye in the air as he made his way back to his house. The feeling of dread at seeing that sign followed him up the walkway. He was hoping they would disperse and give up, but he could hear them talking even from this distance and it didn't seem as if they were going to leave so easily. He pulled out his portable phone to message Brant to be careful when he came home later. He was still typing out a message when he heard a thump on the other side of the door.

He could spy the grinning face of Koffe through the door's window, but it wasn't Koffe who was raking his claws against the bottom half of the door. Nico risked a glance across the street where the onlookers were craning their necks to get a better look. Nico waved again in what he hoped was a "nothing to see here, no dragons, go away" manner, but that seemed like a lot to ask from one wave, so he dropped his hand.

He mouthed the words, "back up" to Koffe while widening his eyes and glancing at the street. He raised his eyebrows meaningfully.

Koffe was a sharp tack, he understood immediately. He leaned down briefly and the scratching noises at the door stopped. He backed away from the door, and Nico walked in quickly and shut the door firmly behind him.

"Any trouble?" Koffe asked in his unmistakable basso profundo voice. He tilted his head towards the street to indicate he was aware of the interaction outside.

Nico sighed as he took the squirming Gus into his arms. "Hard to say. I tried to throw them off, but they seem determined." Nico snuggled the babe briefly, giving Gus a quick kiss on the head and a tight squeeze before setting him back down. He walked over to the living room window and pulled the curtains closed. Gus scrambled excitedly behind Nico.

"I know we knew this day was coming, but..." Nico trailed off despondently, watching Gus play with his shoelaces, tearing them out with his claws. This was a battle Nico had given up weeks before. Fortunately, he had a drawer full of backup laces. A locked drawer. He and Brant were making bets on how long it would stay locked. The currency was exchanging household chores. Gus's dexterity was changing almost daily, and this was a new terror for his dads. Of course, Gus was delighted with it and was testing all kinds of doorknobs, latches, handles, and locks. It was *not* the best time to have a dragon child wandering outside.

"Life will hand you a cupcake and a firecracker at the same time, won't it?" Koffe said philosophically.

Nico sighed again and looked at his friend. "Thanks for watching him. Don't say anything to Brant. I'll talk to him."

"Understood. Don't wait too long, though. He's pretty sharp." Koffe said.

Nico snorted audibly. Koffe had a knack for understatement.

Nico leaned down and gave up his laces to Gus, pulling them out of their eyeholes and handing them to the toddler. Unlike a human toddler, Gus was not prone to putting things in his mouth, but he enjoyed flexing his claws, both front and back. He fell back flat on the ground and started to play a game called "cat's cradle" with the laces, making intricate knots, loops, and patterns in record time with all four of his legs. Nico watched with fascinated horror. *It's going to be a terrible night*, he thought. *I wonder if I could message Brant to stop at the hardware store to get more combination locks,* Nico mused to himself. Those were the only locks that Gus hadn't mastered yet. If he wasn't messing with a lock, it was out of love for his dads rather than a sense of obedience. Just like human children, Gus had no sense that the rules of the house were for his own protection. Nico peeked out the window shade and saw that the crowd was slowly dispersing. He breathed a sigh of relief and waved goodbye to Koffe as his friend headed out the door.

As Nico headed into the kitchen to start some dinner, he pulled out his phone again and saw the half-written message to Brant. He considered briefly and decided to delete the message. It would only stress Brant out when he couldn't ask questions or do anything about it. Brant was a spring-into-action sort of guy. He would only fret at work. Nico decided to talk to him tomorrow if the group outside even came back. After all, they might believe his lie and move on.

A few hours later, and after several delicious fish tacos smothered in mango and lime had been consumed, Gus was settling down and playing happily in the basement with his myriad of toys and Nico was in the living room journaling the changes that he had been thinking about over the last several months. The winter season had been challenging with Gus but also some of the most rewarding of his life. He and Brant had become very close, and watching his friend struggle daily with being a civilian gave him a deeper appreciation for Brant's ambitions. Winter had been a rough month to launch Brant's food truck, Bohunkus, but the few people who had ventured out had been rewarded with some of Brant's delicious cranberry and rosemary thumbprint cookies, then, as the winter had turned to spring, business had picked up even more as word spread.

Gus had become slightly bigger but with it came the tantrums. Despite the communication mat, he was frustrated with having to stay indoors throughout the winter and had taken to zooming back and forth all over the house on his fledging wings as far as they would take him. This had resulted in some destroyed wall decorations, a few dents in the paint and trim, and even some patches of burnt flooring when Gus decided to vent his frustration with a flame or two. Brant lost his temper over that. Although, Nico could admit to himself, hearing your best friend yell, "No scorching Grandma's floors!" to their toddler dragon was pretty funny, in retrospect.

By the time Brant walked in the door at 10:30 p.m., Nico had finished feeding Gus dinner, his own journaling, and his chronicling of Gus's progress. Nico was yawning as Brant nodded wearily at him, closing the side door quickly when he heard the familiar sound of claws scrambling on the basement stairs. Gus was a blur as he leaped into the air, his wings flapping furiously in an attempt to soar gracefully into Brant's chest. What ended up happening was closer to a Wallace flying frog, his claws extended in front of him, perfect trust in landing solidly on Brant's chest, forcing him to stumble back into the door.

"Hey, dude. Were you good today? Give any of the fam any trouble?" Brant was hugging Gus to him but surreptitiously looking around, clearly checking the floor for scorch marks. He looked at Nico, who gave him the thumbs-up gesture and Brant visibly relaxed.

"I'm exhausted. Anything to share from today?" Brant asked, grabbing the extra tacos Nico had left on a plate for him. Parenting meant eating when you could, not when it was best for you. Brant hadn't eaten recently; he was wolfing down the tacos at record speed while looking at Nico expectantly.

"Uh ... no. Nothing major."

Brant gave him an appraising stare. "Okay then. I'm headed to bed. Has he been fed? I can watch him tomorrow; I'm taking the day off." Brant said as he washed his hands at the kitchen sink. Gus was curled around Brant's leg and was tearing his shoelaces out now as well. Brant had bet that Gus would get into the shoelaces drawer in less than a week, and they were already at 5 days. But given the cat's cradle patterns Nico had seen this afternoon, he suspected that he would be losing this bet. That meant he was doing the dishes every day the next week. Rats. Nico sighed inwardly at the thought.

He replied, "He's fed. No major incidents today. Get some sleep, you earned it."

Brant nodded in agreement. "Sounds good."

Brant lumbered off to bed, and Nico followed suit. Gus hesitated, then followed Brant to the master bedroom.

A few hours later, Nico awoke so violently that he sat up in bed, his whole body tense and shaking from sweat. He was breathing heavily as if he had run a long distance in fear for his life. Disoriented, Nico looked around the room in confusion. It took several minutes for his hands to stop clenching the covers. His eyes were so myopic with fear they couldn't focus on finding the water bottle next to his bed. When he did find it, he drank deeply, desperate to wash away the blackened grief that clutched his heart. His head was pounding, his heart was racing at an erratic and accelerated pace, but he had no idea why. His dream had been so bizarre. He grabbed the hair on his head and pulled in frustration. He remembered smoke and a rancid stench. There was a devastation, but what was it? The dream was slipping as fast as it had overtaken him. Nico rose and paced the room, his mind reaching for the details before they vanished.

A vow. A promise, yes. A promise had been made to avoid this at all costs.

But where did that dream even come from?

Chapter 3

The smoke was rising in the morning air from the pit. Huge, white puffy clouds ringed with green and flashes of silver, stark against the blue sky. Gus watched from a distance as the humans gathered the dead into wheelbarrows, scraps of fabric tied around their pitifully small mouths against the overpowering stench, and carried the bodies ungently, dropping them into the deep hole in the ground on the outskirts of the village. A putrid, evil human would drop a torch into the pit and Gus would watch the fire rise slowly. Again.

Xer watched this display with a vast and empty heart. The grief was too large, it swallowed xer whole and left only a frail spine to hold together its claws and ears, its tail and legs. How could xer keep trying? It had been so long in the reckoning of human time, something that dragons didn't bother to measure. What a dragon called a day, a human called a year, so what was this, to xer?

It was not the first time, but someday, it would be the last. Xer swore this again, as if the last swearing — and the one before that, and the one before that — hadn't been in vain. There was a time, in a different country when the ice had covered more of the land, when the presence of different people — something that manifested across all types of humans, wasn't so shunned. Wasn't so hated and feared. Humans were a foolish race. They had such quick brains, so quick that their thoughts leapt like a monkey at a fruit-heavy branch, miscalculating and falling. And instead of choosing a branch closer or stronger, they chose the thin, brittle branch. One that you could barely stand on, and for what? Even as you stood, high on that narrow branch of limited thought with no leaves or other creatures to play and enjoy life with you, they looked down from their branch, spitting and shivering from the cold. Alone.

But most of the monkeys enjoyed the shelter of stronger branches, those with boughs, and built cozy nests. They had each other, they were warm, and they were closer to the ground to forage for food.

Gus loved that time with humans. They hunted with humans, played games with them, splashed in the water, and explored the mountains, caves, and deserts. Along with the wolves and bears, dragons were the best of friends to the humans. For everyone on those lower branches, life was delightful, simple, and full of joy. Gus missed those times and was determined to bring back some semblance of it with xer's affinity, with xer's magics. Gus would never stop gathering a diversity of people, despite the outcome.

But some monkeys just had to stand above the others.

When humans developed the idea of shame, it was only a matter of time before they came for the ones they perceived as different. The women-men. The men-women. The multi-gender. The no-sex. Gus didn't know what they called it; Gus didn't care. Dragons didn't see gender and sex this way. Whatever was seen in nature was to be respected, and nature had a very broad sense of identity. No other species questioned this. Humans decided they had a WAY that was special, something that could set them apart.

What was so great about 'apart'? Gus wondered, for the millionth time. Apart is what led to this. Pointless, tragic, cruel death of xer's beloved ones, now ashes in a pit. Gus had loved those humans. Gus had raised them all and considered those humans family. But these humans standing and watching xer's beloved burn, the ones who were left? They were not kin.

And yet somehow, all thoughts of vengeance had drained from xer's mind. It was not worth fighting with these petty humans about. They would not see reason. They didn't even welcome the mindspeak that the *wolves, bears, and dragons perfected for thousands of years as a way to exchange information. Mindspeak was the deepest way of communicating thoughts and feelings. The fact that humans lost this ability was proof enough of how lost their hearts had become.*

Xer would transform, grow smaller, and hibernate. It was painful and took so much of xer's magic, but xer could only hope that the future held more openness among humans, less judgment and fear. Xer would wait a few hundred years and come back, drawing those beautifully different people close to xer. Xer would try again to show the humans — the brittle-branched, 'apart' ones — that accepting all of their own kind could change their world. Gus had seen it.

Gus awoke from another terrible memory-dream with the caustic smell of death and smoke and *hated* it. Xer climbed the basement stairs, magic still pulsing weakly in xer's limbs, and lumbered over to the human, the plant one, climbing into his lap to get a little snuggle under the soft blue blanket draped over his lap. It was still early morning, the sun hadn't even risen enough to shine in the windows, but the light was brightening every few minutes. The house was quiet except for the groans and creaks of the wood shifting and settling as the outside air grew a fraction of a degree warmer.

"Well, hi there. Rough sleep again?" Nico said softly, a tinge of his own exhaustion evident in his low voice. Nico had been journaling but set aside the black fine-tip pen and battered and stained notebook on a nearby sturdy wooden table. The soft pink and gold colors from the spring sunrise were just beginning to permeate the broad front window, and Gus's eyes closed briefly in clear weariness.

"Do you want some breakfast, or do you want to play first?" Nico's eyes shifted encouragingly to a mat set up on the floor just outside the kitchen. The mat was an irregularly shaped grid made up of hexagonal bases. Each mat was modular, so you could continue adding bases in any direction. On top of each hexagon was a set of round electric buttons, grouped in sets of five. They were clustered together by color, so the red, blue, green, and yellow sections all represented different word groupings.

Nico pointed to the mat, trying to get Gus to use the buttons to communicate. Brant and Nico had both learned that even though Gus could rarely use his mouth to speak, as he had done in the baby supply store, it drained his energy. Gus was never going to speak full human sentences in English. Since they were in unfamiliar territory on how to communicate, the mat was their best option at the moment.

Gus glanced at the mat, which he normally enjoyed, but didn't move. Nico pointed a hand, encouraging Gus again. "Will you at least tell me if you are hungry? It's good practice." Nico smiled gently at Gus. Gus sighed and clambered out of Nico's lap. Xer hunted for the correct button to tell the plant man what xer wanted. Xer located the yellow button and pressed it four times, deliberately pausing each time to punctuate xer's intent.

Nico laughed from the living room. "Okay, okay, I get it. 'Hug, hug'. I hear you." Nico stood from the soft armchair and came over, scooping up Gus in his arms.

"Oofta. You are getting big." Nico commented, straining a little to shift Gus to his hips as he made his way back to nestling down. He adjusted his pajama top and yawned wide.

A short while later, Brant's shuffling slipper noises came out from around the corner, and he flopped down on the couch heavily. This was becoming more of a regular thing for their little family; on the rare mornings that they could, all three of them would sit in the living room during the early hours and try to catch up on the latest news. Brant yawned expansively; his arms outstretched as his whole body took the opportunity to wake up. His legs were straight out in front of him, toes pointed, and eyes closed. He followed by tilting his head to each side to stretch his neck. His pajama bottoms rose slightly as he slid his feet out of his slippers and rotated his ankles left, and then right. After a few minutes, he spoke to Nico, still rubbing the sleep from his eyes. "So how did it go yesterday?"

Nico shifted Gus, putting him down to go into the kitchen to start some hot milk for boiling. On more difficult days like this one, Nico liked making a hor-chai-ta at home. He was working a bit later than usual today, as the gardens closed once a month in the morning for the gardeners to do some routine maintenance on the ponds. The indulgent drink would, hopefully, take the edge off what he was about to tell Brant.

The blend of horchata and chai recipe was an instant favorite in their house, but it was incredibly rich. This meant that factoring in the drink meant also factoring in a workout in the basement. He could especially use one today, as he needed to not only combat the effects of the extra sweets, but to also fight the exhaustion from his terrible dream. He was tired at even the thought of a shower, much less a workout, but he did enjoy the feeling afterward.

As Nico pulled the ingredients from the impressive spice cupboard, he told Brant, "Well, the masses have finally found us. I spotted five people across the street yesterday. Signs, chairs, very nosy. Definitely not the neighbors. I talked to them to find out what they knew." Nico was boiling the milk and tea leaves, adding in the crushed ginger and cardamom pods from the mortar and pestle. Brant was staring absent-mindedly at the front page of the newspaper. The photograph of the mayor had been taken just as he was raising his hands during a speech. When Nico spoke, Brant abruptly put down the newspaper and replied in a tense voice, "How worried should I be?"

Nico set down the spoon he was using to stir the ingredients and reached for the sugar.

"Some stupid radio program decided to try and 'make it fun' to find Gus, I guess. The people outside suspected something but I tried to throw them off the scent. We'll have to see if they come back. There was a little old lady who was the main person I talked to." Nico added the sugar and tasted it. It reassured him in a way he could not describe. It was like seeing an old friend and holding them in your arms. The relief cut deep.

"So, keep an eye out today, got it," Brant said, sighing heavily. "I mean, we knew this day was coming, I had just hoped to come up with a plan before then. I guess I thought we'd also have found a more sophisticated way to talk to the little guy than 'cheese' and 'uppies.'"

He stood and walked awkwardly over to the stove because Gus had wrapped around his leg tightly. His lumbering and shuffling steps made Nico smile secretly to himself. They hadn't come up with a plan, it was true, but the time they had spent was still precious, nonetheless. Brant tasted the chai with a big spoon and nodded approvingly.

"This is delicious. Maybe add more cinnamon next time." Nico's eyes lit up briefly and he nodded, his eyebrows raised at the idea.

"Was there... anything else?" Brant looked at Nico as he asked, his eyes lingering briefly on his friend's slumped shoulders, the dark circles under his eyes, and Nico's general listlessness. This was not an uncommon sight back in their early days with Gus, but it had been a few weeks since Brant had seen Nico this haggard.

Nico started to feel the crippling grief from the dream all over again, but stubbornly, most of the details continued to elude him. He could only recall burning, and death. He could feel the intense sadness pressing down like an impossible weight on his shoulders. He almost had it...what was that awful feeling? It was similar to judgment, but worse. Nico realized in horror the word he was searching for. It was persecution.

Nico winced visibly, and Brant waited to see if he would speak. Brant was concerned for his friend, but one of the important aspects of living with someone was giving them emotional privacy, even when you were standing right next to them.

Nico spoke finally, and the words came out cut off, almost distant. "No, nothing else." He decided to change the subject before Brant could press further.

As Nico started towards the second-floor stairs, stiff as a steel rod, he muttered, "I'm going to go change so I can work out and then take a shower. You got Gus?"

Brant scooped up the grinning Gus into his arms, his muscles bulging with the effort. He nodded sympathetically at Nico.

Brant managed to throw Gus slightly in the air, making the dragon smile further and wiggle the ever-growing ears.

Brant was still playing toss-the-baby when his phone rang a few minutes later. It was their friend from the casino, Paula.

"Hey Paula. What's going on?" Brant said, forcing himself to sound carefree. Gus had started to follow Nico downstairs as Nico headed to the basement, but Brant knew that the kid would only disrupt his workout. Nico needed to clear his head, and Brant would help him to do that, even if his friend wasn't ready to talk about what was on his mind.

Brant grabbed Gus by the midsection and took the dragon into his bedroom. He didn't like to encourage it, but bouncing on the bed was a good distraction. Gus clambered up the tall bed frame and ran across the mattress to his dad to get thrown. Brant would throw Gus in the air, Gus would bounce a few times, flapping wings slightly, then come back to Brant to get thrown again.

Paula could hear the low growls through the phone and laughed at the mental picture. It was a trick she had needed to use a time or two in recent weeks.

"Just checking if you two need help today."

"Oh, thanks so much, but we are good today. I'm home and Nico's going in late."

"You two need to get out more! Do something other than obsess over parenting," Paula said, her grin evident through the phone. "It's not healthy to be cooped up so much. I'll come by and do relief in a few days, let you two get away to go watch the dragon boat practice races or something."

Brant paused, unsure of how much to share. If their address had been leaked to the radio station staff, how had they gotten it? He dismissed his paranoia immediately; he trusted Paula. She had risked more when they were relative strangers, and she didn't deserve his mistrust now.

"As much as I love the idea, we did have some general nosey public who showed up yesterday. I wasn't there but Nico talked to them. They may show up again, so sadly, no waterfront people-watching until we find out what's up."

Paula blew out a breath of disappointment. "Well, we knew this was going to happen eventually. He was spotted a few times when you guys took him on that hike, remember? In the car and on the trail? It's just human curiosity. But if people are showing up at the house..." Paula trailed off.

Brant understood perfectly what she was implying. It was fine if the Multnomah residents gawked from a distance, but finding the house was going to be a big problem. They needed a solution, and in the meantime, some boundaries.

"Thanks for checking in, Paula. Talk to you soon." Brant hung up at the same time as Gus had landed for his umpteenth bounce. Gus looked at Brant with such open love and delight that his heart contracted painfully. His love and protection for the little dude had only grown to an impossibly large size since they met. He couldn't articulate his feelings if he tried. He was still considering the implications of their house being found when a strong knock came from the front door.

My Baby Grows

<u>Attitude</u>: (Scale of 1–5, 5 being happiest.)
Very surly, 2.

<u>Behavior</u>: A tantrum coming on is indicated by color changes along spine, low guttural growls, a swishy tail that slaps the ground.

<u>Changes in weight, body shape, color, extremities</u>:
Gaining approx. 5 lbs a month. Body shape is growing out slowly, approx. 1 1/2 in/mo. Color remains gray with

green-mottled flecks. Claws grow slowly, 1 mm/mo.
<u>Communication</u>: Uses preset buttons on mat for basic requests and feelings.
<u>Changes in motor function, diet, and sleep</u>: Marked improvement in dexterity. Claws are excellent now at grasping but tend to manipulate into being held as if they don't work. Diet is still birds, but has expanded slowly to supplemental foods.
Steals and enjoys cheese puffs and chocolate/marshmallow cream easter eggs. Sleep was good for 6 mos, but lately very fitful, crying out in the night and restless during naps.

CHAPTER 4

Knock, knock, knock! came from the front door, the one they never used. Using the side door was always easier to access the car from the house. The knocks had a curt and unfriendly sound to them.

Knock, knock, knock! came again, this time more aggressively.

Brant came out of his bedroom, entering the room quietly and stealthily, gesturing for Gus to stay back. Gus sat perfectly still on the bed, forehead furrowed in confusion. Brant's face was alert and hyperaware, his eyes darting back and forth in threat assessment. Nico had come up the basement stairs, his face shining with sweat and his eyebrows creased with worry. Both of them heard a stern male voice call from the front door.

"This is U.S. Army Lieutenant Colonel Malcolm Hatworth. We want to speak with you about your...ward."

Brant gestured silently to Nico to close his bedroom door so Gus couldn't come out. Nico slid into Brant's bedroom and Brant could hear a low and urgent whispering as Nico asked Gus to remain quiet. Nico was back in a moment, closing the door behind him. He was sweaty but presentable, and they both stepped up to unlatch the front door lock and greet the stranger.

Brant and Nico both took in who was at their door: a white guy in his mid-60s with a haircut so short and sharp it could cut glass. He stood 5'9, very trim, with a stern expression in his eyes and a resolute set to his jaw. He looked as if he could play poker and sweep the board.

Brant spoke first. "Hello, Lieutenant Colonel. What brings you to the neighborhood, especially at this early hour?" he said, quite coolly. He was aware of what the colonel *said* he wanted to talk about, but he wanted to dig a little further. Military higher-up's came in two flavors: dance around the point or get right to it. He hoped this man was a straight-talker and would just come out with it. Since Nico couldn't read what was passing between the two military men, he just stood behind Brant's shoulder, but as Brant spoke, he straightened up taller and crossed his arms in a clear display of what-do-you-want.

"I think you know why I'm here, son, and I'd like to come in and talk about your... new responsibility." He moved forward a few inches, almost imperceptibly, but as he did so, it was enough to set off Brant.

"With all due respect, Colonel, but now is not a good time," Brant said brusquely, matching the colonel's step. Nico uncrossed his arms and decided to try another approach. Maybe the colonel would agree to leave if they were a bit more cooperative? He couldn't risk a glance at Brant to assess, so he ran a hand through his hair and relaxed his stance.

"Colonel, we do appreciate the visit, but Brant is right, now is not a good time. Have we broken any laws?" he said, smiling in an open and trusting manner. Brant glared at Nico for a second before turning back to the colonel, stony-faced.

The colonel ignored Nico completely. "Son, threats to national security usually don't come at a good time. It's in your best interest to work with me before the magical delegation," — he wrinkled his nose in clear derision — "arrives. I thought

I could reason with you first, but maybe you are more foolish than you look." He delivered this in a disapproving-father, condescending tone.

Brant smiled broadly now, and Nico knew that Brant was about to say something very reckless. There were few things Brant enjoyed as much as being underestimated, and though his line of work was very healing for his past, Brant still held a healthy dose of fiery temper at the ready when the occasion called for it. Whether he meant to or not, Nico knew that the colonel had just made an occasion.

"Oh, so you think the magical delegation hasn't already been here?" Brant was grinning openly now. "Because as a matter of fact, they paid us a visit just last week and told us that their jurisdiction on the subject of..." he paused, unsure if he wanted to reveal more, "our charge superseded any claim, priority, or threat that *they* deem as legitimate."

The colonel shuffled his feet slightly but didn't break eye contact. Brant had been bluffing but recognized that the colonel had not conferred with the magical tribunal in the Northwest territories, or he wouldn't be at their door trying to bluster his way into their house and gather information. Brant's grin grew even bigger. He had the upper hand now and wasn't giving the colonel an inch.

"Soooo, thanks for stopping by. Unless there's something else?" Brant's smile had turned dismissive, his eyebrows raised at the question. Nico stifled a laugh and turned it into a cough. While the colonel said nothing before leaving, only giving a curt head nod before turning and walking stiffly down the front porch stairs, Nico suspected that Brant had struck a nerve. There probably were some politics at play here that they weren't aware of when it came to the rights of magical creatures. Hopefully, Brant's refusal had bought them some time to figure out what to do next.

Brant shut the door firmly and locked it before turning to Nico.

"Well, that was a disaster sausage wrapped in a puff pastry. I would say we are truly fucked at this point. Once he checks what I said — and he will — he will be back. National security — fiddle-faddle." Brant said in a huff as he stormed back towards his bedroom. He calmed himself slightly by taking a deep breath and exhaling as he went to open his bedroom door to check on Gustopher.

Gus looked up at Brant innocently, his claws tangled in a cat's cradle, quietly playing with an enormous pile of impossibly knotted shoelaces. The locked drawer next to Brant's bed had been pulled out completely and overturned on the floor.

Nico peered over Brant's enormous shoulder and snorted a little.

"Wait, does this mean you lost the bet since he went for your drawer and not mine?"

Brant turned and glared at Nico as Nico laughed.

The next few days were tense, to say the least. Brant was rage-baking in the kitchen, which always resulted in a mixed bag. On one hand, it meant that he was mentally working through something and didn't like being interrupted, though it was a pain in the butt for Nico to avoid the kitchen completely. On the other hand, a steady stream of delicious treats was often left out, and this resulted in some of Brant's incredible new creations mixed with old classics. The latest concoction was an absolute winner for the night customers of the cookie truck. It was a salted dark chocolate pomegranate cookie. Though it was very rich, the dark chocolate paired with the pomegranate tang was just heavenly for Nico. He concluded, as he always did, that letting Brant have the kitchen was the best move. *Am I an enabler?* Nico thought to himself. *Oh, well.*

Because of all the baking Brant was doing, Nico did the dishes, as it was clear that Brant needed the extra support right now. Brant muttered to himself as he baked, and Nico could make out the words "go to my sister's" and "tactical plan" a few times. Nico knew that Brant would share his thoughts eventually. Brant was great about collaborating on co-parenting topics. The security of Gus had come up several times, and Brant never imposed what "he thought was best." He offered up a suggestion, and they discussed the pros and cons together. For two people who had never parented and barely knew each other, the honeymoon period had been pretty sweet so far.

On the third morning after the colonel had paid them a visit, Nico and Brant were both up early, giving Gus a quick bath and feeding him before Paula showed up to watch Gus so they both could go to work. Brant's anger had died down and now he was so distracted that he kept leaving half-finished tasks all over the house. A laundry basket filled with rumpled clothes was next to a pile of neatly folded towels in the living room. A cold cup of coffee sat lonely in the kitchen, half-drunk. A storage tote from the basement had been brought upstairs and rifled through, the contents strewn across the floor, the lid propped next to it.

So, when they heard a friendly knock at the side door, none of them were expecting to open the door and find a stranger in a lab coat standing there.

Time seemed to stop for a moment. Brant was standing at the sink, trying in vain to get Gus to stop playing with the faucet and bubbles so he could wash Gus's claws and tail. Nico had a toothbrush in his mouth, brushing with one hand while he shuffle-walked, his foot half inside of his right boot, perched and ready to be laced up. Nico had just opened the door for what he *thought* would be Paula, not even bothering to look up, as he was focused on his unbalanced foot.

He heard an unfamiliar voice say awkwardly, "Hello. My name is Dr. Michael LaBorn. I'm from the Multonmah BioScience Society. May I come in?"

Nico stared at the stranger. He was a tall Black man in his mid-40s. He had a pinched, unpleasant look on his face, and he was wearing a lab coat. He had the irritated look of a person who had just discovered their rental car wasn't filled up with gas before starting a trip. He was accompanied by two others behind him, also in lab coats. To Nico's eyes, they looked like junior scientists. There was a woman to Nico's left and a man to his right. Both of the junior scientists had a look of nervous excitement.

Nico pivoted to look at Brant and Gus. His mind felt so sluggish. He hadn't had another horrid dream as he had before, but his dreams had still been like molasses, stodgy and slow, and it had made his days the same way. He still hadn't told Brant about his disturbed sleep, dismissing that it was of any importance. But now, it was taking him forever to absorb what he was seeing. Brant was there, yes, at the sink, with bubbles and water everywhere, his bright green kitchen gloves were always adorably matched to the green flecks on Gus's back. But where was...Gus?

The dragon had vanished. It looked as if Brant were taking an upper-body bubble bath with himself. The same look of incredulous astonishment on Nico's face was reflected on Brant's face. He was just as shocked to find his arms empty.

Brant turned slightly back to the sink and reached out a hand to the spot where Gus had been. He ever so gently moved his hand through the air where Gus's head should be, and nothing was there. He covered up his intent in front of the strangers by reaching for the faucet and turning on the cold water. There was a small growl from the sink, and Brant startled back. Brant turned the water to warm and let it run for a few seconds before he turned back to address the strange trio. Brant's face now wore the same expression as when he had greeted the colonel.

"I'm sorry. We are having some backed-up plumbing issues, and you caught us a bit off guard. We weren't expecting *you*; we were waiting on a friend to come by to help us with...cleaning out the garage." Brant looked pointedly at Nico, who surreptitiously pulled out his phone while turning briefly away from the side door. Brant moved smoothly over to stand in front of it, blocking the scientists from coming in.

Mr. LaBorn's frown deepened. He said, "I apologize for the abrupt arrival, but it's extremely important that we talk with you. We've heard from our military liaison that you have a specimen of extreme value, and we would like to work with you on beginning a series of experiments. We've had high success in treating some conditions with a glandular secretion we found in our lizard test subjects. I'm sure you can see the value in starting as soon as possible," he sniffed slightly with displeasure and arrogance. He clearly wanted to be elsewhere.

The two scientists behind him, however, looked thrilled and intent with their visit. Brant recognized the expression: it was greed.

Brant had officially had it with people coming by to tell them what to do. The colonel had been bad enough, and now he was watching his best friend suffer for some unknown reason that Nico wouldn't talk to him about. He hated not being able to help. Now his baby dragon had vanished, and some arrogant, pushy scientist was coming to his door to demand access to Gus, aka "the specimen," and run EXPERIMENTS on him? Who did these people think they were? Salt and sugar, if the words national security come out of this guy's mouth... and worst of all, he didn't have a *plan* for what comes next. Brant hated not having a plan.

The junior scientists were looking extremely nervous now as Brant's expression turned downright angry. Brant was taking calming breaths loudly through his nose, looking up at the ceiling and away from the visitors. Nico had texted Paula with the code they had worked out in case something started to go off the rails. The code was "pickle juice." It had only taken Nico a few seconds to send, and it would direct Paula to proceed with caution and take their lead when she arrived. Nico could see her pulling up out front from his vantage point, where he also saw, *Oh, great,* more onlookers gathering on their street with more signs and chairs. It was shaping up to be a very bad day.

Brant's face had dropped to a stony blankness. Oh, vines and roots, this was BAD. Normally Brant reveled in being confronted because he knew he could hold his own. But Nico had seen his lip curl when the guy had said "experiment" and there was no putting that rootball back in its pot.

Brant's tone was even as he spoke, "We don't know what you are talking about, and even if we did, showing up here unannounced and uninvited is inappropriate. A lieutenant colonel from the Army was here a few days ago — your contact, I assume? — but he was *also* turned away. And unless both of you have legal cause or *warrants* to search my house or property, you are not welcome here. I've got..." he glanced at the sink for a fraction of a second, "other things to worry about."

Paula was just walking briskly up to the door, pushing past the junior scientists and striding in. She took in the scene of the chaotic kitchen, the look of shock on Nico's face, and the anger brimming on Brant's. She said, looking strategically at Brant with confidence, "So do you want to get started?"

Brant replied, "First in here, then in the garage. Sure thing. They were just leaving."

He shut the door in Mr. LaBorn's face and closed the curtain over the small window in the side door.

They all stood in silence, waiting for the scientists to leave. As soon as it was safe, Nico walked over to the living room window, pulling the curtain closed. Brant had rushed back over to the sink, calling softly, "Hey, kid? Are You there?"

Paula was watching them both, baffled but waiting patiently for an explanation.

Gus reappeared at the sink out of thin air, and Paula yelped. Gus's ears were folded down and he was shivering. His eyes were downcast, and he looked exhausted. He was panting and his front claws were gripping a sponge tightly. Brant scooped him up from the sink, wrapping him quickly in a nearby towel. He ran to the basement, jumping down the stairs two at a time. Paula and Nico stared at each other. Paula was pointing at the empty sink, her mouth open in shock.

She said quietly, "What was that?"

"I wish I knew." Nico said, confused.

"Is that something he can do?"

I don't know. I guess so."

"Why did he look so bad when he...came back?"

"I don't know."

"Has he done that before?"

"I don't think so. I don't know."

"What are we going to do with a baby dragon that can *disappear*?"

"I DON'T KNOW." Nico practically yelled. His nerves were completely shot, and Paula's interrogation wasn't helping.

Paula quickly softened and apologized, "Okay, I'm sorry. I'm just in shock. Poor little kid looked so shaken up. I hope Brant is okay, too." Paula said, starting to pick up around the house absent-mindedly. Paula was good like that; she liked to always be moving and helping out.

Nico sat on the kitchen island bar stool, trying to take it all in. He was just so tired. His brain couldn't stop seeing Gus vanish before his eyes. His heart kept panicking over and over. He needed to see Gus. He stood suddenly and walked down to the basement, where Brant was jiggling and comforting Gus. Gus was no longer shivering, but he still looked so worn out. He could barely keep his eyes open. Nico walked over and stroked Gus's ear gently. Gus opened one eye and let out a little rumble. Then his eye shut again like a doused fire, and he was fast asleep.

Brant looked up at Nico, his face was tight with anguish.

Nico nodded sympathetically. Brant tucked Gus into his bed, fluffing extra blankets around and burrowing him in so deeply you could only make out his face and ears. They walked quietly back up the basement stairs and shut the door.

Gus slept for the next five days.

CHAPTER 5

Late March

During the days and nights that Gus slept, Nico and Brant decided that one of them should be with Gus at all times until he woke up. There were too many unknowns. Was this sleep more like a coma? How long would it last? How had Gus vanished? It seemed to be a self-preservation reaction, but they had no one to ask. Would Gus fully recover, or would it leave some damage or scarring?

When the onlookers had seen the science research team show up, their suspicions were confirmed, and so an encampment had formed as the word had spread. More people had arrived with signs, offerings, and candles. Some had even set up altars. The neighbors hadn't said anything yet, but Nico could see them getting hassled as they went about their own routines and knew it was just a matter of time before they approached the house to ask them to intervene.

Brant was in a temper all the time; he was so on edge and snappy that Nico spoke to him only when needed. Brant tried stress knitting, but it didn't help. Both were just so worried about Gus. Nico had not been sleeping well before the invisibility incident, but now his anxiety had shot up so high that he didn't think he'd gotten more than a few hours each night that Gus was still unconscious. They had left food next to him, toys, and even brought his favorite plushie bumblebee out from behind the china hutch where Gus had tossed it one day, but nothing woke the downcast little dragon, his face peeking out from the blanket fort Brant had built.

To at least try to take the pressure off of Brant, Nico went out to talk to the gathering crowd while Gus remained unconscious. Nico didn't do well in large groups, being the introvert that he was, but he wanted to continue his practice of speaking with strangers. He couldn't expect Brant to speak for him on every occasion, anyway.

As Nico approached, he discovered that they were a mix of fearful and reverent. There were two types of people there: some had doomsday signs declaring that "The End is Nigh" and "There's no Aliens in the Holy Scrolls" whereas the other type of people were passing out snacks, joking, laughing, and held signs such as "We love you!" and "Teach us!" It was evident that some of them had watched too much *Doctor Who*. Did they think Gus was here to save humankind? Nico shook his head at the thought.

It was evident that magical equaled extraterrestrial to some of them, and Nico guessed that the lack of understanding magickind was contributing to the fear and mistrust.

Nico spied the older woman from the last encounter and made his way over to her. As he got closer, several people pressed in close to listen. When Nico gestured for her to step aside with him for privacy, she obliged.

"So," she said, a note of triumph in her voice. "I knew you were helping the beast! Does it talk? What does it want? Why haven't the cops come to take it from you?" she said both demanding and eager. Nico was taken aback. He thought she was the reasonable one, but he underestimated her desire for scandal.

Nico sighed heavily. "Look. It's...HE is not an alien. He is a baby dragon, and his name is Gus. We legally have the paperwork and rights to keep him, and he is in good hands. He's no danger to anyone in Multnomah and certainly isn't here to save or destroy humanity. We can do that all on our own," he said, a note of bitterness evident in his tired voice.

The woman snorted in disagreement. "There's no need to take that tone with me, young man. A dragon? That sounds mighty dangerous to me. You might judge it to be safe, but who's to say? Especially as it gets bigger, hmm?" She was fostering suspicion, and she knew it. Nico was disgusted that such a person would capitalize on spreading lies, or that she continued to act as if Gus didn't have an identity or feelings of his own. He tried a different tack.

"If you really are worried, you can take it up with either the mayor's office or the magical community's tribunal elders. And just to be perfectly clear, stay off our property and don't harass our neighbors. Quiet hours in this neighborhood are strictly enforced," Nico stated firmly, bullshitting the way he'd learned from Brant. After all, if Brant could make things up to protect Gus, why couldn't he? He left without making eye contact with anyone else.

Nico stomped back to the house and went straight to his room to try to calm down. He could hear Brant downstairs, singing a soft lullaby to Gus, and it broke his heart that people just outside their door were hailing Gus as a new prophet or a global threat when he was just a little toddler who threw tantrums and loved cheese puffs.

Brant went to work the night shift at the truck that evening while Nico stayed with Gus. He had made a taco salad to eat in the basement while catching up on journaling, curled up next to Gus to share his body heat.

Nico was about to take his fourth bite when Gus's eyes popped open, disoriented. Nico was so shocked he scrambled up, knocking over everything nearby to crouch in front of Gus's face.

"Hey there. It's okay. You are at home. It's okay. It's Nico," he soothed, speaking low and calmly, though his heart was beating a mile a minute.

Gus blinked a few times in rapid succession, pushed out of the blankets, stretching his front claws first, then arched his back like a feline and stretched his back half. He stared at Nico, his face solemn, but the color of his skin and general tone looked better than it had in days. Nico watched Gus and gave the dragon some space, but stayed close in case he had a relapse.

He was just taking out his phone to send Brant a message that Gus was awake when Gus walked over to the center of the basement and stood very still. Nico watched as the colors began to ripple down Gus's back. But instead of the iridescent colors like the incident when he was a defensive fireball at the casino, these were shimmers of brown and pink, alternating and coursing through him at a faster and faster rate. Finally, Gus let out a rippled pulse of crackling sound that burst from him all at once in every direction. There was no change in the room, but Nico *felt* the change in ozone in the air. It reminded him of the aftereffects of a lightning strike.

After this, Gus turned and looked back at Nico, his mouth open in his toothy grin, back to his old self again, and scrambled to the overturned taco salad, picking out the cherry tomatoes and popping them between his claws happily. Nico sat in shock and happiness for a moment before suddenly reaching out to scoop up Gus and squeeze him as tight as possible. He laughed from sheer relief and said quietly, "I don't know what's going on with you, and we love you no matter what. But DON'T EVER DO THAT AGAIN. YOU SCARED US TO DEATH."

After getting Nico's call, Brant came barreling in the door exactly 23 minutes later still wearing his apron and serving gloves. Nico and Gustopher were curled up in the living room, Gus was sprawled across Nico's lap, and they were watching a television show about angels and demons working together to avert the apocalypse. The show was a favorite of Brant's as well, and the sting of seeing his family watch his favorite show quickly melted when he realized they were watching an older episode. One of the deceptive things about Brant was that despite being so muscular and bulky, he could move very fast when he needed to.

Gus heard him come in and jumped from Nico's lap towards Brant, using his fledging wings to assist him in flying across the air. The living room looked into the dinette area and had a clear view to the side door, so Nico could hear the audible "OOF," and "Easy there!" when Gus launched himself at Brant. Man and dragon collided and fell to the floor in a heap of laughter, hugs, and flapping ears, tail, and wings. Brant was overjoyed at seeing Gus back to his old self. He was murmuring something urgent in Gus's ear, and Nico caught the tail end of "ever again!" which made him laugh, as he recognized the sentiment.

After a good half hour of coddling, fussing, and feeding, Brant and Nico put Gus in the basement to have a house meeting about what they were going to do now that Gus was back to "normal." Normal for Gus, anyway.

They were parked in the kitchen at the island so they could keep an ear out for Gus downstairs and any shenanigans he might be up to. Nico was brewing some hot water for tea, and Brant had pulled out a few cold sandwiches that another food truck vendor had thoughtfully offered when he saw Brant closing up early for the day and dashing off. Brant also pulled out the batch of classic cinnamon shortbread cookies to finish off their meal.

Once they had laid out the food, Brant began.

"I don't know about you, but I was NOT prepared for the last few days. I'm sorry. I've been rough to be around. We both knew the crowd outside would eventually show up, and I knew the military would come knockin', but the Gus highs and lows at the same time was just..." he trailed off, shaking his head. Nico sympathized completely.

"I hate to add to our troubles, but there's a little bit more." Nico continued. He filled in Brant on the strange sound pulse that Gus had done after waking up, as well as the conversation Nico had had out front with the onlookers, and Brant looked even more baffled and tired than before.

He waited for Nico to finish before he spoke. "The people outside — while an annoyance and a growing issue if things get out of hand — aren't my primary worry. None of those nosy Nellies wants to risk arrest from trespassing; they are too scared of Gus and what he might do. And given how many other eyes in the neighborhood are watching them, trust me, they won't be storming the front door." He looked contemplative for a moment, considering. "No, it's the audio pulse you are talking about that has me wondering. Was that a, I don't know, a bat signal of some kind? Is he calling someone? or something?" His eyebrows shot up, hopeful. "Do you think Remi and the hockey boys might get called back? We could use the help."

Nico didn't have any answers either. He shook his head. "No, I doubt it, though I miss them, too. If Remi wanted to be found, he would've shown up already. It felt different, somehow. It wasn't the pull of the gut that his other magic felt like. You know, that protective feeling? This was more like a megaphone." He smiled at Brant. "Maybe it <u>was</u> the dragon version of a bat signal. Can you imagine? What if Gus really does know a half-man, half-bat?" They both started grinning at the thought. The levity only lasted a moment though, as reality crashed back in.

When Brant finally spoke again, there was a heaviness to his tone. "All of these things happening at once really got me thinking. I have been hesitant to talk about this, because I hate this idea, but we are SO far out of the fellowship, we might as well be Boromir." He took a deep breath, not meeting Nico's eyes.

"I think we should consider turning Gus over to the magical tribunal. The little dude would be protected from the military sniffing around, and while they might not know any more than we do, at least he'd be with other magical creatures," Brant said mournfully. "I don't know what sort of asylum Gus would have, but I can't imagine the military has jurisdiction to claim him." He looked at Nico to gauge the reaction.

Nico was shocked. He knew that the stress was intense at the moment, but Brant was always the first one to say how important it was not to quit. Every time they watched a movie or a video about someone going through a tough time, Brant always said encouragingly, as if the people could hear him, "Don't give up!" Nico felt as if his feet had been kicked out from underneath him. Why was his friend acting like this? Was this about Gus, or something else? Was this a remnant of the war? The more Nico thought about it, the angrier he became.

"Absolutely not. We don't know the politics of the magical world or how they see Gus. We don't know if they are any better equipped to raise him than what we've learned. I have half a book already of notes and progress updates! And most importantly, Gus chose US." Nico started considering his sleep troubles, and while he was recalling the horrendous dream he had had a few nights prior, something clicked. These changes going on in Gus, was that dream actually Gus's and not a figment of Nico's mind? Was he in Gus's dreamscape? There was something about it that had felt so foreign and strange. His own dreams had familiar themes of anxiety, of neglecting a garden or plant, or of his family judging him for transitioning. Nightmares of identity and trying to date. This other dream was so completely different than the tone of his life, maybe that's because it wasn't...his life? The idea was staggering but Nico kept silent. If Brant wasn't fully committed to raising Gus with him, then there was no point in telling him about how Gus's magic was changing.

Brant's expression was full of helplessness, and he played with a cookie briefly, breaking off pieces into a pile of crumbs. "Well, I have no idea how we can make a plan with just the two of us. We can't drag Koffe and Paula into this, they have lives of their own. We don't know who we can trust. Running away has never been my style." He sighed heavily. "I just need one *simple* day, you know?"

Nico heard the defeat in Brant's voice. He went over to pat his friend on the back reassuringly.

"I know. I get it. Between what's going on out there, "Nico gestured at their door, the motion encompassing all the mounting pressures, "and what's going on in here," he gestured downstairs to Gus and continued, "we really are out of our depth. But we are stronger together, and I'll bet that Gus is still here because this is where he feels safest."

He paused slightly, considering if he wanted to share his suspicions about the dream.

"I don't know if the question you are asking is the right one. Instead of asking, 'Should we do this?' or 'Is there somewhere better for Gus?', we should be asking, 'What do *we* need to do to help Gus thrive?'"

Brant nodded solemnly as Nico spoke. He looked relieved that Nico had brought up this perspective. Brant spoke again, with a hopeful tinge in his voice, "Well, that's a good way to approach it, but we still need some logistical changes around here. Until we come up with a stronger plan, I can at least start to build an area out back that's more reinforced from prying eyes, but still gives Gus some room to roam if we aren't taking him somewhere. We can put some reflective material in the truck windows so people can't see him in case worst comes to worst and we do have to flee. And we can install some cameras to alert us when people come to the side door."

Nico added, "See, now we are talking. And Koffe can help with a bunch of that; you know he's wild about electronics."

"Yeah, he is. I'll give him a call." Brant had pulled out his phone to call Koffe when there was a knock at the side door.

"What was I just saying?" Brant said, sarcastically. "Not one. single. day," he muttered through gritted teeth. Nico looked at Brant, worried again, but Brant conceded begrudgingly, "You are right. Don't quit on the little guy."

As Brant moved to answer, Nico gestured that he would go downstairs and sit with Gus. Brant waited until Nico had slipped quietly down the basement stairs and shut the door firmly before opening the side door.

Standing before Brant was a mismatched trio. There was a petite person who was almost half his height and stood barely four feet tall. They had androgynous features, bright green eyes, and a riot of color in their mohawk hair which sparkled and shimmered as it caught the light. They were quite elderly; Brant guessed they were in their mid-80s. They reminded Brant of an old punk rocker or a pixie.

Behind them stood an enormous hairy man. He had his arms crossed and wore a hostile expression. His beard was dark purple. Brant suddenly had a vivid recollection of a customer he'd met once outside of the bakery he used to guard. The guy had gone off on a rant about the obvious difference between something called Hollow Purple and Midnight Purple. He had described Hollow Purple as the gorgeous blue-purple color of a summer sky that hasn't quite hit the witching hour, whereas the jackass had scoffed that anyone could mistake it for Midnight Purple, which was closer to Eggplant. Brant liked the turn of phrase about the witching hour so much that it had stuck in his head, even if the person it had come from was an arrogant windbag. Brant guessed now that the hairy man's beard was a shade of Hollow Purple. He wore a ring in his nose with a red stone at the base.

To Brant's left behind the pixie was a tall woman who was clearly a vampire. She was over six feet tall and had a Mediterranean complexion. Brant deduced from the still-scarlet blood stains on her shirt and sleeves that she had fed recently. While she had the same chilling personality that Remi had had upon meeting Brant, this woman's smirk was utterly humorless. It scared the shit out of Brant. So did the punk rocker. Brant could just tell, however, that the bearded dude was a teddy bear.

The pixie spoke with formality in a thin, raspy voice. "Greetings. My name is Lezahtun. My colleagues will share their names if they wish. We are aware that you are warding a dragon. We make up part of the magical tribunal of the Three Sisters mountain territories. We summon you and your ward for a viewing and to receive judgment in the town hall at the full moon summer solstice. The tribunal will make its assessment at that time."

They stared at Brant, expressionless. The bearded dude huffed a few times but said nothing. The vampire continued her smirk and was now looking Brant up and down. He was not unprepared for this moment, and he decided to try some tactics he had learned in the last 12 months. Ever since the fae had come out to humans, Brant had taken the view that while he wouldn't seek any of them out, he wasn't going to run away screaming, either. He had hoped to not run into any of them again after Remi — who had been plenty — but he was cautious enough to at least research how to interact with the magical folk, especially since Gus had come into their lives. Make no offers, strike no bargains. Don't offer your name. Make statements, and frame suggestions as a theoretical musing. He replied, "The young dragon has claimed us. I wonder what will occur at the tribunal."

Lezahtun had a tight, wry smile. They could tell that Brant was careful not to divulge anything of value. They replied, "The tribunal's purpose is to guide all magical creatures through disputes and...displacements. The question of the dragon's origin must be determined, as well as whether or not," they gave a wider smile now, and Brant could make out some *very* sharp teeth, "the 'young' dragon is in an environment that is safe for the rest of Multnomah." They gestured vaguely in the air. Brant took "the rest" to mean humans. He wondered exactly how many fae there were.

He did *not* like the mention of this town hall. They were going to need someone with knowledge of the workings of the fae to help guide them. Brant cursed Remi's abrupt departure for the millionth time. Where the heck did Remi go, anyway?

Brant spoke carefully now. "Humans at a magical tribunal sound like a dangerous endeavor. I am confident that a liaison or legal counsel would be a wise strategy."

Lezahtun nodded solemnly. "We are equally confident in the wisdom of legal counsel. There is a person who is a historian/ambassador between humans and the fae. She will arrive in a drone bee lifespan[1]. Partings," she said, tilting her head slightly and turning to leave.

Brant had a question burning in his mind, and before he could stop himself to think it through, he blurted it out as the trio turned to leave, "Does this mean the military will back off?" and realized his mistake as soon as he spoke. The vampire woman unnerved him so much that he had asked a direct question. The pixie turned back, their satisfied smile like

---

[1] A drone bee's lifespan is 55 days

the sound of a predator trap snapping shut. Brant winced at the mental image.

"If the military presence troubles you, an arrangement of trade may take place," they said expansively, spreading their arms wide in acceptance.

Brant was relieved that a deal had not been solidified. He suspected the pixie was being gracious by giving him a chance to get out of it. *Holy shit, this is stressful,* he thought. Nico would've hated it. He replied hastily, "No arrangement is needed. Partings," he echoed, eager to end the interaction.

The three of them left and Brant shut the door firmly, locking it and pulling the curtains shut. Just for good measure, he turned off the light as well. *Damn,* that had given him the willies. Despite his bravado at just agreeing with Nico not to quit on Gus, how in the big bakery in the sky were they going to handle a magical tribunal? Brant felt a deep, unfamiliar anxiety in the pit of his stomach. His fingers itched to whisk a meringue, to work some butter into dough, or even to zest some aromatic citruses into a lovely pile of food confetti.

Instead, he took a few more minutes to gather himself and go tell Nico that they had all been summoned.

Chapter 6

A few days later, Nico was dozing off and on, sitting on the couch with Gustopher in his lap. Brant was working late in the kitchen, creating a batch inventory of his classics so he would be well-stocked for the weekend.

The sun had dipped beyond the horizon and the dusky spring sky was a stunning palette of pastels in pink and peach with tinges of purple and blue. Brant and Koffe had plans to install a clever window treatment that would allow them to have privacy in the lower part of the window that was visible to the street, but still let in light in the upper portion. At the moment, Nico could only see the sky if he pushed the curtain aside to see it, careful not to move in such a way that would disturb the dragon or allow the onlookers to see Gus.

The onlookers had been showing up every day, and while their numbers were growing and they were a nuisance, so far there hadn't been any fights, protests, or disruption to the neighbors. There was an uptick in trash, though. Tonight the street had cleared, and Nico breathed a sigh of relief.

He stroked Gus's head between his ears, and his eyes fluttered as he tried to keep them open. Gus was letting out little rumble snores, and after a few minutes, Nico finally succumbed and drifted off.

Xer was sitting in an open circle among humans. An exchange of trade was underway. In the distance were tall tropical trees with their sunbursting spikey leaves. The soft white sand felt delightful between xer's toes with granules so small and fine they looked like the sparkle of dew across an early morning. The rising sun was radiant in the sky but tempered by the gentle ocean breeze. The waves crashed almost lovingly in their heartbeat pattern at the shore, and xer felt calmer with each passing minute. An intoxicating waft of meat was tempered by the sweet smell of tropical fruit on the breeze that drifted by.

The humans were exchanging hides, herbs, spices, jewelry, and tools. It was a good trade, as the visiting tribe had not been seen for many seasons and their ship had brought a bounty of items to share. The elder of the island tribe, a woman-man of great wisdom and renown, was known for their connection to xer in particular. Xer visited these islands frequently, as xer loved the openness in which they lived, their happy manner, and their embrace of human diversity. The women of this island guided them, made decisions about exploration and harvest, and presided over disputes. Xer's animal companions on the islands were the whale and the turtle. Both had lived as long as dragons and enjoyed a relationship with humans of respect and cooperation.

Xer was given a large gift by both tribes of fish and birds as a display of honor and xer's position of being close to the elder of the tribe. Later that evening around the bonfire, as the drummers pulled out their instruments, xer started a low consistent beat in xer's throat, setting a baseline for the musicians to begin the dance. The feast and dance lasted well into the early hours, and the elder and Gus retired to commune and share visions of the other places of the world that xer had been to. The spiritual connection between the elder and Gus was one of sacred importance and would guide the elder in the years to come. Knowing about how other cultures were progressing was vital for trade.

Xer loved it here and visited as often as xer could but was needed in many places. In just a few short weeks, xer would leave and find the next tribe to connect with. Strengthening the connection with humans was not just about pleasure, but something all dragonkind needed. A tribe in the north had started to have different ideas about dragons, claiming they were weak for embracing humans that weren't male or female. They had begun to praise one type of human over another, as if they didn't each have their own strengths and weaknesses. Gus had been growing concerned at the thought of isolating one type of human from another, and xer was grateful that the island peoples had no such ideas. It was why xer fostered the connection here by visiting often.

Once xer had shared the vision of this northern tribe's attitude with the island elder, xer sneezed a little fire — as xer often would — after a mindspeak. They smiled at xer with true affection and laughed at the sniffles, snorts, and the trail of smoke coming from Gus. Their friendship was stronger than ever.

Nico awoke with a start, the dream vivid in his mind, and looked down at Gus. Gus was awake and staring at Nico, uncommonly still. Nico could still feel the grains of sand between his feet and taste the smoke in his mouth from when he...no, *xer* sneezed. Astonished, Nico looked down at his hands, holding up his fingers to make sure they weren't claws. Unlike the nightmare he had had a few weeks ago, every detail of this shone in his mind. It had been dazzlingly real. Nico was recalling the sensation of feeling truly gender fluid, which was a strange concept to him. He had always felt firmly rooted in masculinity, even before his transition. But now....now he was rooted in Gus's point of view.

The only way he could think of it was like being at the threshold of two vast ballrooms with soaring ceilings, opulent decor, and flooded with light. He pictured himself standing in a small antechamber between them. The ballroom to his left was femininity and the ballroom to his right was masculinity.

And he, in the middle, could dance and play in one and effortlessly glide into another. He could even swap items from one ballroom to another. There was no limit to expression in these joyous, strong, complex spaces that led to further rooms, creating new identity palaces. If this was how Gus felt about himself... *No, about xerself,* Nico corrected, then they had misgendered Gus for too long, and Brant needed to know right away.

Nico adjusted Gus to address xer directly. He was shaking his head, side to side in disbelief before half-whispering, "Is this really happening? Did that happen to you? How did you share that with me? Is that really how you see yourself?"

Gus reached up with one claw and touched xer's head deliberately, once, before reaching out to touch Nico's head, softly and only once. Xer had sent Nico the memory directly, yes. Nico chuckled softly and pulled Gus into a hug.

"Seems as if you do have other ways to communicate. No wonder you don't like the mat buttons." Nico laughed, then was serious again. "I need to talk to Brant."

Nico rose from the living room to find his friend in the kitchen, carrying Gustopher on his hip as he went. Gus wriggled slightly and Nico set xer down. Gus ran up the stairs and headed straight to Nico's room, presumably to rifle around in places xer shouldn't go. Nico left xer to it; he had more pressing things to discuss with Brant.

"Hey. Something happened, and I know it's going to sound bonkers, but please hear me out."

Brant's shoulders tensed as he went to put down the bowl and spoon he was holding on the kitchen island, but he said nothing. He gestured with a small nod for Nico to continue.

"I had a — I guess, a vision just now that Gus sent me while I was napping. More like a memory? Not sure what to call it. It was *very* vivid. I felt as if I were there, completely. I was inside Gus's mind. To be honest, I also had a horrible nightmare a few nights ago that was pretty bad, but I didn't connect that it was related, until this." He gestured wide with his hands to encompass both experiences.

"I can't remember much of the nightmare, unfortunately," Nico followed up, frowning.

Brant sighed heavily. He said, "I knew something was up last week, but didn't want to press you. You don't remember the nightmare at all?"

"No, just fragments. Awful stuff. Burning bodies. Grief. Pain. Really, really deep pain," Nico said, struggling to even bring it up. Brant's eyes turned sympathetic, and he said, "After the last few days, I'm expanding my sense of what's possible with the little guy."

"That's just it — or, just another thing. Gus isn't a guy. Gus is what we would think of as gender fluid. Gus thinks of themselves as 'xer'."

"Okay. Well, that isn't the important bit, is it?" Brant said dismissively. "What was the vision-memory thing about?" he pressed on.

Nico was upset that Brant of all people could be so hurtful about how Gus thought of xerself. *How can that not be important?* he thought. *It's only the basis of one's identity.* Nico was distraught but still thought it was vital to share the vision details in case it shed some light on Gus's other behavior recently. Nico outlined the broad strokes to Brant of the island, the elder, the trade, and the relationship Gus had with the elder. He emphasized that the elder was also non-binary, but Brant barely seemed to hear.

"You don't think the identity of this elder and Gus being similar is connected in some way?" Nico finished, leaning forward slightly, trying to will Brant into seeing the relevance.

"Not really," Brant said, running a tired hand through his hair and turning to put some of the baking ingredients away.

Brant wasn't getting it, but Nico wasn't about to let this slip. If Brant couldn't understand the importance, how would anyone else?

"Gus sent this vision to *me*, Brant. A trans man. I think there's a real connection there, and I certainly think that both of us constantly misgendering Gus must've bothered him — I mean xer — enough not just to clarify but to send an entire technicolor experience to me while I slept!" Nico's voice had risen as he was visibly flustered. Gus came barreling down from Nico's room upstairs and galloped to rest at his feet. Nico felt a stab of sympathetic grief at how Gus must've been feeling this whole time, comprehending but still being misunderstood. This was a feeling he knew only too well from his family.

Brant tossed a dirty whisk in the sink making Nico jump. "Look, we've got four kinds of threats out there. The military might have already planted listening devices around our house. The science people may very well show up with a form stamped "epidemic' and whisk Gus away. That punk rock fairy might be able to walk through a wall for all I know. And that's if one of the throngs out there doesn't throw a firebomb through our window just to get a peek at 'the alien'!" Brant's voice had risen now, too. Both of their faces were flushed, and Gus was running back and forth between their legs and whining.

Brant looked down at Gus and took a deep, calming breath. It only partially worked.

"I got other things to worry about than the gender identity of a dragon," he said tightly.

Nico's heart dropped as Brant said these words. He stood and walked stiffly to the living room, grabbed the journal where he had been cataloging all of the events of the last few weeks, and threw it down on the counter. Brant hadn't been allowed to read it before, but the message was clear: read this.

Nico grabbed his coat, opened the side door, and walked out.

Brant watched his best friend storm out after he had said the most terrible thing. He knew it the second the words had come out of his mouth. He had trivialized the two people he loved the most, and he felt sick. Gus had gone to the basement and was quiet.

He gently lifted the journal, wiping his flour-covered hands on a towel, careful to make sure there wasn't any residual spice on his fingertips before turning the pages. He could see Nico's steady hand, scrawling the details he was tracking for weight, feedings, milestones, poop times, nap time, and mood chart. He even included how many teeth Gus had grown. When he read about the details of the visions Nico had been experiencing, Brant felt even worse.

Nico had been very invested in observing Gus to the smallest detail, which Brant didn't have the patience for. Seeing the progress over the months all at once, especially how many bad nights and tantrums there had been, shed some light on why Gus might be frustrated in trying to communicate with the two of them. Starting a vision with something as basic as how Gus viewed himself made sense, in that light. *Xerself*, he corrected silently.

Brant was reading through the latest entries of the visitors that kept showing up when Nico came back home. It had been about an hour and Nico didn't make eye contact with Brant as he put his coat on the hook on the wall just behind the door. Nico began to shuffle to the stairs when Brant spoke.

"Hey, man. I'm really sorry," he said softly. " I got worked up. This isn't an excuse, but as you know, it's been a bad couple of weeks. My mind has been racing and it's got me overwhelmed. I miss the strength-in-numbers thing of my squad. I didn't mean what I said. Calling Gus a 'he' just became a habit. But habits can change, and bad ones, especially, *should* change. If Gus is a 'xer'... is that how you say it? With a z?" Nico nodded reluctantly.

"Cool. 'Xer.' I can do that. It *is* important. I got no excuse. I'll do better," Brant finished.

Nico relaxed substantially, turning to face Brant and looking him in the eye.

"So you think there's a connection about the whole gender diversity thing?" Brant prompted encouragingly.

Nico shrugged and said, "Not sure. Let's see what happens next. I'll try to get every detail written down from that and see if anything new comes from it." He paused before saying, "And thanks."

They nodded briefly at each other and smiled at the return to equilibrium.

Later that night, as close to midnight as Nico could stand, he tried to call the phone number that Remi had sent them shortly after he'd bolted last September. There was no answer, but Nico left a brief voicemail. He hesitated but asked Remi to call them back. He hung up with little hope that the vampire would. Wherever he was and whatever he was up to, they were on their own.

Can now hide in plain sight by going invisible, but only effective for a short period of time. Causes a significant magic drain for several days, like a coma, causing Gus to sleep deeply. Xer also stands still and arches xer's back up, sending out an audio-sonic wave burst after rippling colors across their back for about 10 sec.

Gus has sent me a vision. It in is in the past, hundreds of years ago? among transgender and nonbinary people who were revered for their wisdom and connection to Gus, in particular. Set in a southern set of islands. Abundant food source. No evident technologies or metalwork, crude transportation.

Chapter 7

April

Nico and Brant spent the next few weeks discussing all the new developments and the options they had open to them, as well as sharing what they felt was important to Koffe and Paula. Their friends both offered to help in any way they could, which was a relief for Brant, especially after the arrival of the tribunal and their announcement of the town hall. Brant and Koffe dedicated several evenings to the new security measures and making sure they had window treatments to protect their privacy. The two men reinforced locks both inside and outside the house, added a fenced gate to the backyard, and installed cameras at the front door and the side door.

The garage was cleaned out and the emergency supplies were checked in case they needed to either run or go through a lockdown. Brant was taking no risks when it came to what the military might be up to. He went through the house every day looking for listening devices that could be planted by prying ears. He was diligent and though it took its toll on his mental health, Nico could see that it gave him something to do with his frustration and feelings of insecurity about the future.

Brant also made a concerted effort to correct the habit of misgendering Gus. He sat down cross-legged one evening and spoke softly to Gus for a long, long while. Gus watched Brant the whole time, occasionally batting at Brant's legs playfully. Nico couldn't hear the conversation, but it seemed to reset them both profoundly. There were fewer tantrums from Gus and xer was generally less fussy after this, which helped the entire household greatly.

Gus had sent another vision to Nico, just as detailed and vivid as before. This second vision was set in a northern climate across a permafrost tundra. Gus's visions were a cacophony of stimuli all at once for Nico, and it took him a few minutes to adjust to the sensory overload. He could sense how the days were beyond a description in English or in Spanish of the word "cold". The chill was so instantaneous, so punishing and impassive, it felt as if the air were an impartial deity, unaware of the damage it did with a single flick of its wrist.

Nico-as-Gus was standing in front of some humans who were being targeted by the village. Gus was guarding the huddled mass of frightened humans, protecting them. The tribal elders were swayed by the crowd of angry people who were growing angrier and shouting that it was best for the "others" to leave. Nico-as-Gus had met with the elders of the tribe, but they were unflinching in their suspicion. They were the ones who had fostered an environment of exclusion and mistrust, encouraging the villagers to cause this casting out.

Gus could see the art of the heavy ironwork all around the settlement. There was a protected grain store within the walls of a fortress. Symbols of the new worship were everywhere, the telltale cross hanging ominously from high on the wall. Gus had noticed that wherever this symbol showed up, humans made things more and more complicated, especially for those who didn't follow the new faith of that town or village. A growing schism that had led to so many migrations, banishings, burnings, and death. The rise of hate and othering had led to a mistrust of dragonkind. Gus was not as welcome as xer had been before and was seen as taking sides among the humans. Xer had heard of some dragons being hunted for their association with musicians, wanderers, tinkerers, and craftspeople; anyone who was defying the new beliefs.

Nico awoke from the memory/vision and felt the wet tears of repressed grief on his face. It was early morning, but Nico could see the rays of soft sunlight as the star climbed in the sky. The sight comforted his aching heart. Normally, this was Nico's favorite time of year; the explosion of new life was all around and impossible to ignore. The gardens were at their most beautiful and Nico was always busy with the groups and tourists that flocked there. But these visions from Gus weighed heavy on his heart. What was it that Gus was trying to convey? Why was xer sending these visions now? Why wasn't Brant receiving them?

Nico had even more thoughts crowding his head, but instead, pushed them back to the distant corner of his mind and trudged to the bathroom to get ready for work. There was no use in pressing the issue; you only got blooms from steady watering, light, and patience. Nico was used to waiting. Patience was a gardener's best attribute.

One topic that Nico was not patient about in the slightest was the magic tribunal. In this, both he and Brant agreed. This was the biggest concern on their radar, and the looming date of summer solstice gave Nico spikes of anxiety every time he thought about it.

They had talked extensively but realized that they needed more information about how the tribunal process would go, the position they were legally entitled to take, and how best not to piss off anything that could kill them before they could make a decision. Gus was clearly talented at defense (little fireball of joy) and evasion (invisibility) but the toll it took on xer was substantial, and Brant and Nico couldn't test Gus's abilities without risk. They continued to have more questions than they could answer, and it frustrated them both.

Nico was especially anxious that the ambassador being sent might not help their situation. He would feel better if he knew their background or had a chance to do research, but it was not as if he could walk up to any of the human-magic liaisons on the street. He didn't even know how many there were in the world, much less Multnomah. Or was the ambassador sent from another place to help out? Nico had looked up the drone bee life cycle and found only an estimate of 55 days. So this meant they didn't know exactly when the ambassador would arrive. Nico decided to throw himself, as usual, into documentation.

He cataloged as much as he could of the visions, the details of Gus's growth and new abilities, the patterns of the crowds outside, as well as his reflections. Journaling had always been a safe outlet for his thoughts and feelings, and his notebook had become so full of confidential happenings that he began carrying it with him everywhere for safekeeping. It was stuffed full of loose bits of paper; he often didn't have his journal right near him or was too tired to retrieve it, so inside were scribbled napkins, torn pieces of paper bags, receipts, and sticky notes.

It had been a little over three weeks since the magic delegation had come by, and Nico had just begun a journal entry one morning. Brant was preparing a catering order of cupcakes and cookies for a little girl's birthday party and had been bustling in the kitchen for several hours, designing what he mumbled were the 'Wee Free Men', tiny, blue-bodied figures with electric red hair. Nico had the day off and was nestled down in the living room, Gus squeezed in — barely— next to him on the couch.

Gus had grown a bit in the last several weeks, and xer's colors had started to deepen along the spine and on xer's claws. Instead of a medium grey with small green spots, the gray had begun to darken, and the green had started to spread further across xer's body. Gus was now considerably darker in the green shade, almost as evergreen as the trees outside the window. Xer was now the size of a Saint Bernard dog.

Xer had grown less clumsy in the last few weeks as well as displaying better coordination. The fledging, chaotic flights had smoothed out, and Gus could land now with barely a sound. It was both beautiful and frightening how big and yet how calculated Gus's movements were. Xer's personality was still as loving as ever with their little family, but when it came to playing with toys, Gus showed a keener focus than ever before. Gus's appetite had doubled and xer was even sleeping with a new and eerie stillness Nico had never seen before.

He wished for the thousandth time that he knew more about Gus's physiology and why xer was going through these changes.

Patience, he thought to himself. *Patience is what wins in the end.*

Nico was only a few sentences in when there were two alerts simultaneously that someone was at the side door. He checked the alerts on his phone at the same time that Brant did. The security system allowed the outside camera to send updates instantly to their mobile phones, and Nico was grateful for the precautionary measure. These days they couldn't be sure who it would be now and what their demands were.

Nico and Brant instantly shared a glance, both of them in motion. Brant wiped chocolate frosting from his hands to his apron, straightening it as he walked over to the side door. Nico was leading Gus to Brant's bedroom and asking xer to lay low. Gus nodded but broke into a big grin, xer's tongue hanging out in a relaxed manner. Nico shook his head when Gus tried to follow him back to the living room, putting his fingers over his mouth in a "shh" gesture. Gus sat contentedly on the bedroom floor, looking around for some toys to play with.

Nico stepped back into the kitchen, nodding in affirmative to Brant.

Brant opened the side door to a group of four strangers, all looking at each other and then back to Brant in a very confused manner. Brant scanned them quickly, looking for poster board signs, lab coats, or anyone in uniform. What he saw was what appeared to be a random sampling of strangers. *I would bet Nico five chocolate brownies that this is related to the bat signal,* Brant thought wryly.

There was a balding gentleman who stood about 5'9 and slouched somewhat in a crumpled suit with a sheepish, embarrassed expression. His complexion was pallid, and he wore an out-of-fashion pair of glasses pushed up on the bridge of his nose. Everything about him screamed accountant or small-town banker. There was a younger Black gentleman with freckles and a beard who wore a cautious expression. He was the tallest and stood at the back at around 6'2. He wore a cardigan and had his hands tucked in the pockets. He looked as if he were about to lead a literary discussion at a local community college. To Brant's left was a nonbinary white person in their late 20s with a windswept-styled haircut. They stood about 5'10 and wore bright red lipstick, snake earrings that looped the entire ear, and matching bright red painted nails. They wore a red latex vest and a charcoal-grey flowing skirt. The person to Brant's right was an Indian man in his late 30s or early 40s. He wore a turban, and a large musical instrument case was resting next to his feet. He stood about 6 feet tall and when Brant caught his eye, the stranger's eyes crinkled as a slow smile crept across his face.

Since there didn't seem to be a clear leader and the way they were acting led Brant to presume they didn't know each other, Brant spoke first. "Can I help...all of you?"

The small-town banker spoke, hesitation evident in his voice. "I'm not sure. I think I'm supposed to be here, but I just couldn't tell you why."

The tall man in the cardigan from the back piped up, "Yeah."

Brant examined the strangers more closely. "Soooo, you were drawn to my house, but don't know the reason?" he clarified.

The first stranger who had spoken shook his head as if he were trying to work through a particularly difficult trivia problem. He looked up at Brant with a sincere expression.

"It's like this place feels *right,* you know, but at the same time, I don't know you at all. I have no good reason to be at this door. I felt a pull to this place, and at first, I drove in the wrong direction, and it started to fade. But I drove north, and then west, letting the 'signal' I guess, get stronger. Eventually, the pull was so strong, I just knew where to go when I got to the Multnomah city limits." He paused when Brant snorted at the word "signal" but continued in an amazed tone. "I just know that I got in my car from Missoula, Montana, and drove straight here."

Astonished, Brant said, "Are you all from Montana?"

The others piped up one at a time, saying that they had come from New Mexico, Utah, and Washington.

The banker spoke again, "I feel like I'm supposed to be here, you know? at this house, specifically. This feels as if I've...arrived? God knows what I'm going to tell my wife. She's been calling since yesterday." He gave a laugh of disbelief.

The realization had come to Brant when he had opened the door and seen them, but he decided to confirm the hunch. Nico nodded at Brant, trusting whatever move he wanted to take next.

Brant switched to a diplomatic tone.

"Would you all mind waiting here for a minute, please? Don't talk to those crowds over there, though. They won't be of any help, trust me." There was unanimous nodding from the strangers, and they all began talking amongst themselves as Brant shut the door softly. He walked over to the master bedroom and opened the door, Nico trailing behind.

"What is it?" Nico asked anxiously.

"I have a feeling this is like what happened when we first met Gus, only on a bigger scale. Remember how we felt really drawn to xer? Remember how the hockey guys were interested in tagging along? How Paula felt when she first met Gus?" he theorized, sitting across from Gus, who had stood up from where xer was curled up in Brant's closet and was circling excitedly around their feet.

"Hey buds. I got a question for you. Remember what we talked about the other night?"

Gus nodded, barely able to contain xer's happiness. Nico waited for Brant to fill in the gaps.

"I asked you to tell me point blank, to answer my questions about any new surprises, at least to the best of your knowledge. So here's my question: There are some strangers outside: not magical, not military, not scientists. Just some well-meaning strangers who don't know why they are here. Some of them came a long way. Did you bring them here with your magical mind powers or your little sonic superblast?"

Gus nodded enthusiastically. Nico rolled his eyes at Brant's choice of words.

"Is it safe — for you or us — to show you to them?"

Again, more nodding.

"Can they be trusted?"

At this, Gus calmed slightly and sat still. Xer closed xer's eyes and concentrated. After a few seconds, Gus opened xer's eyes and beamed at Brant, nodding again in the affirmative.

"Last question, pumpkin butt. Can they resist whatever magic you're using to pull them here, if they want to?"

Gus nodded again, even more excited than before.

"Okay, okay, I get it. You are excited. Give us a few minutes, okay? We need to let them know what's going on before you come out," Gus jumped up on the bed, straining the frame and mattress. Nico glanced at Brant. "I'll stay here and keep Gus company."

"Good idea," Brant replied dryly.

Brant walked back out and opened the side door for the second time.

"Hey, everyone. I've got some answers for you. If you are comfortable with it, please come in." He gestured to the dinette area off the kitchen in a welcoming manner. The area was a regular dumping ground of baking supplies, soil, trowels, laundry, and anything else that came in or out of the house. Freakishly, it happened to be clean-ish at the moment, and the relief was visible on Brant's face as they gestured encouragingly for them all to come in. The group walked in and sat around the large wooden oval table, exchanging hesitant glances. Every chair was full, so Brant addressed the group standing. Once everyone was settled, he began.

"Here's the thing. We think we know why you all were drawn to Multnomah, and specifically to our door. My roommate and I met someone about six months ago who has some unusual...qualities. Gustopher is quite adept at bringing people together — I'll explain this more in a minute — and I think that's the *what* you are drawn to. I've spoken to xer and my roommate, Nico, who you see here," Nico gave an awkward little wave as he came out of the bedroom, "and we want you to know, first and foremost, that what you are experiencing is the result of a persuasive kind of magic. You all know about the magical folks, right?"

Brant paused and everyone around the table nodded in the affirmative. Two of them started to look alarmed. Brant raised his hand reassuringly.

"First things first, you are safe here. While Gustopher does have magical abilities, Gus has no intention of harming you, and as a matter of fact, is very excited to meet you all. Now, regarding the magic. It *can* be resisted if you decide you don't want to be here. I went through this exact thing six months ago, and after I met Gustopher, I decided to just go with it. Now Gus lives with us, and my world is much better for it. I only mention this so you know that I made the same choice you are faced with now.

I just want you to know that if you feel uncomfortable, it's completely your choice to leave."

The worried brows and tense shoulders that Brant could see relaxed visibly, and someone let out an audible puff of relieved "whew." He could imagine how trying to weigh that choice without the visual of Gustopher was challenging. He was glad he had had a cute little gargoyle to look at, back when he was faced with this decision. He could hear Gus in the other room getting impatient by bumping against the door and decided it was time to do the introduction. Everyone looked towards his room.

"So this is your last chance to walk out if you would rather not be here. Again, it has to be *your choice*. I'm about to introduce you to a magical creature and once I open this door, there's no unwhipping that meringue."

Hesitant acceptance in the form of head nods turned to immediate confusion, and Brant added hastily, "I'm a baker. You get used to the metaphors. Everybody ready?"

There was a murmur of agreement and nodding, and Brant shook his head, no, once.

"Not good enough, I'm afraid. We're going round the table; you tell me your name and your decision."

One by one, they answered.

The banker spoke first, as before. There was a squeak of anticipation in his voice. "My name is Koker F. Rathbone, III. I agree to the introduction and I'm excited."

The person with the snake earrings and red latex vest spoke next. Their voice held a note of uncertainty. "I'm Laszlo Toth. I am here of my own free will."

The man in the cardigan spoke third. His voice was sure and low. "Sylvester. Let's do this."

Brant turned to the Indian man next and was greeted by a warm smile. "My name is Oded. I consent to the introduction."

Brant locked eyes with Oded the musician and felt an amused undercurrent to his reply. Oded flashed him a cheeky wink so fast that Brant thought he'd imagined it, if not for the sly grin spreading across Oded's face. Oded was admiring him, giving him an appraising look up and down. No one saw the exchange, everyone else was now looking fixedly at Brant's bedroom door.

"Okay, then. That settles that." Brant cleared his throat to bring his focus back. He walked over to Nico and whispered, "You ready?"

Nico nodded and took in Brant's blushing face. "What's up with you?" he said, the smile evident in his voice.

"Nothing!" Brant said furtively. "Can we focus, please?"

"Of course," Nico responded, but he was clearly tickled to see his friend so flustered.

Brant strode over to the door, cracking it slightly. He gestured to Gus, opening the door wider.

Chapter 8

Gus was uncharacteristically calm as xer walked slowly out of the bedroom to sit on the floor of the kitchen. Xer made long, deliberate eye contact with each stranger.

There was a choked cough at the table, and Koker stood suddenly.

"It's all right. Xer is harmless," Brant said, soothingly.

"Why do you keep saying that pronoun, 'xer'?" asked Laszlo, puzzled. They kept their eyes on Gus the entire time.

Brant replied smoothly, "Because that's what Gus is; neither male nor female. Gus is a dragon and has a special connection to Nico. Xer communicated that pronoun and thinks of xerself as gender fluid or beyond the binary as we know it. Do you have a problem with that?" he said lightly, but Nico heard the steely undertone. *That's not fair,* Nico thought to himself, *it's not as if Brant was super comfortable with it at first, either. I suppose,* Nico considered, *it's because of his discomfort that he is more protective about it now.*

Laszlo shrugged noncommittally, "Not me, man. I play with the gender binary daily like a ping pong ball. I go by 'they,' personally. I just didn't think a...sorry, what is Gus again?" they said, distracted.

Nico could almost see the hackles on Brant's back calm down. Brant went into education mode and stood a little closer to Laszlo, his hands gesturing in animation. Gus had remained very still, xer's eyes watching with an open curiosity. "When we first met Gustopher, we thought xer was a gargoyle, and we thought xer was a 'he,' but we were wrong on both counts. Parenthood is very humbling," Brant finished, perfectly deadpan. Nico snorted at the gross understatement.

Sylvester asked thoughtfully, "What made you think those things?"

Brant replied, looking closer at Sylvester to see how he was taking in the situation. The tall man seemed a little flustered but curious. Brant warmed to the subject now that they weren't panicking or looking for an angle, just expressing genuine interest. "Well, first of all, xer's skin was greyer at the time — this was back in September, when we found him — I mean xer! Anyway, it was after a mafia shoot-out in the street. Nico and I just happened to both be in a hardware store, see," Nico cleared his throat conspicuously. Brant took a breath and paused. "I'm sorry. You are the first people to not freak out at the sight of Gus, and we've been on the defensive for a few weeks now."

Nico saw Oded look at Brant with an adoring smile and glanced over at Nico. Something passed between Nico and Oded. Nico could read the instant affection the musician had for Brant and the babbling currently going on. Nico smiled back and gave a small head nod at Oded as if to say, *Yes, he's always like this.*

Brant continued, oblivious. "Anyway, Gus originally had a stone-like texture on xer's skin. Gus's features were smaller, especially the horns and claws. The body. Xer just looked more like a gargoyle," Brant shrugged, recalling the first meeting with affection. A grin spread across his face at the thought. "Now, Gus is looking more like what'd you'd picture a dragon to look like from our fairy tale books. And the misgendering...well, that's my fault. We know better now."

Nico saw Oded mirroring Brant's grin, looking at the baker with open flirtation.

Brant finally addressed Oded, turning to address him with the faintest flush to his cheeks. "We are still working out the nuance of why Gus has attracted you all here, though we do have some suspicions. We used to think that Gus tended to attract good men with a field of persuasion and protection. But there's a broader range of people now, not just men," Brant nodded to Laszlo, and Laszlo nodded back, "so we will need to go back to the drawing board on that one." He clapped his hands together decisively.

"Now that you've all met Gus, you are welcome to stay and ask a couple more questions, but we do need to get to our jobs this afternoon. Gus will be watched by a friend of ours," Nico looked questioningly at Brant, who gave a nod of affirmation and pulled out his phone to contact Koffe. Brant began stepping away, but Nico could still hear the words faintly, "Can you come early? More developments..." as Brant stepped into the living room.

Meanwhile, Gustopher had finally stood and walked slowly over to Oded and pawed at his lap, one claw resting gently on his leg. Oded laughed softly to himself and reached out to pet the top of Gus's head softly, scritching behind the ears. Gus closed xer's eyes languidly, reveling in the hard-to-reach spot that was usually reserved for xer's closest family.

Koker, Laszlo, and Sylvester had pushed back out of their chairs and stood, putting the chairs back in. The sound of scraping wood and shuffling echoed in the small space, and Gus went to Nico for reassurance. Nico petted xer gently, his heart clenched in anticipation. He felt as if he were waiting for their judgment, their fear. The strangers had all handled it pretty well, given that they had come from so far away. But was it all too much? Was it too weird? He could hear Brant trying to fill in a bit of detail to Koffe in the other room. He felt awkward sitting there, but he wasn't leaving Gus's side. He waited, trying to focus on being patient. The group of them stood huddled and talking by the side door, all except Oded, who remained at the table, a serene expression on his face.

Nico could hear them discussing in low voices. Koker was visibly the most excited, his feet shuffling in literal impatience. He kept glancing at Gus in affection. Sylvester and Laszlo were more reserved. Nico watched as Sylvester crossed his arms over his chest while Laszlo ran a nervous hand through their hair.

After a few short minutes, Brant turned back from his call and caught sight of Gus at his friend's feet, and Oded, unmoving and content at the table. Brant's expression turned...unguarded, almost giddy. Nico stared openly at his friend looking so smitten and happy. He had never seen Brant so...silly. Brant was crushing on the newcomer. Why wasn't he starting a conversation?

Brant cleared his throat and composed himself. Nico and Oded exchanged glances. Oded seemed to know that Brant was flustered and was enjoying causing the discomfort. Nico thought this was the best thing to happen to *all* of them in weeks.

The small group clustered by the door fell quiet, and Koker stepped forward and spoke.

He started in a soft but assured voice and said, "I can't speak for the others, but I'm all in to help or support however I can. I've been an accountant for over 30 years and never thought something like this could, or would, ever happen to me. I'm thrilled to be here and would like to contribute. I don't want to break any persuasive magic I'm under," he laughed at the thought, "so I think what I'll do is get a hotel room in town and spend tonight considering the details." Nico could feel Koker's openness and willingness. It was plain that whatever was happening next, Koker was in.

Sylvester spoke next. He said with real admiration in his voice, "I remember hearing some buzz about something big and magical happening out this way, and I think it's dope that you all have formed this bond." His tone turned cautious. "Now, I do have some obligations back home. I work with the homeless population in Seattle, and I need to make sure they are in good hands before I uproot my life. Give me a day or two to check on things. But...yeah —"

Nico looked alarmed, raising a hand to interrupt Sylvester.

"No one is asking you all to stay here. We thought you were just here to meet Gus," he said. Nico turned to address Gus, who was now walking around everyone and bumping their legs. Well, in reality, Gus was now so tall he was bumping their hips.

"Gus, is this what you want? More people around?" Gus looked strangely at Nico and didn't respond.

Laszlo asked, "Can't they speak?"

Brant replied shortly, "It's xer. And it's complicated." He sighed. "Look, I need to finish this catering order and we can explain everything later, for those of you who want to know more. Nico and I do need to talk about this...new development. Why don't you all —" he grabbed a notebook from the side hutch and tossed it down on the table with a pen — "please write down your names and contact info here, and I can call you all later after I'm done with the bakes and delivery."

After ten minutes of logistics, Brant was just shutting the door on the four reluctant strangers who were off to find accommodation. Nico suspected that from how buzzed they were from meeting Gus, they'd probably head straight to a restaurant to talk further. Brant and Nico had both asked for their strictest confidence, and all of them had agreed not to speak of Gus to anyone else.

Koffe was due to arrive any moment, but Brant needed to touch base with Nico. He sat with a thump in one of the barstools. Nico sat next to him, turning his chair towards Brant. Brant gave Nico a serious look. "We are going to need to re-think this whole thing. This changes the game. Again." Brant rubbed his face briskly, his eyes scrunched up as he tried to release the tension at his temples.

Nico watched Brant with a playful expression as he said innocently, "That Sikh guy in particular seemed to take a shine to Gus. What do you think of him?"

Up to this point, Nico and Brant had never discussed their love lives. It seemed like something that would've happened sooner, but when you are delirious from sleep deprivation and trying to keep up with a growing — and far too cunning — magical dragon who has no evident way to communicate, some things just fall to the side. Brant blushed furiously and shuffled his feet.

Weakly he said, "Now isn't the time to check out hot guys—"

Nico grinned like a gambler scooping up chips after winning a poker game. "How interesting! *I* didn't say he was hot. *You* said that. Okay, great. Now that we've established the hotness of Oded —"

Brant broke off Nico with a moan of protest at the sound of the musician's name. "Listen up. I'm not going to be mooning over some hot Indian guy" he paused briefly, clearly remembering Oded's knowing smile. " You know what? Fine. Why not? It's not as if there are more important things going on," he said sarcastically. "I'll ask Oded out. We'll fall into bananapants love and skip through the meadows, and he can play the oboe or whatever was in that case, and I'll feed him cupcakes and the sun will always be shining. Are you happy?" Brant huffed and crossed his arms across his chest.

Nico beamed at his friend. It was good for Brant to stop worrying for once and just enjoy the changes. There were undoubtably more things afoot with Gus, and they needed to be flexible with those changes and not fight it. *A young sapling, not a stout oak,* Nico thought. He felt as if he were channeling Remi briefly and felt a stab of sadness at missing his friend.

"Sarcasm doesn't always look good on you, you know. And actually... yes. I know we have some real threats at our door. We don't know how much longer we will have with Gus, or what might happen next. But that's *all the more reason* to take the joys we can as they happen. That guy is clearly into you. Gus likes him. You know that's always been the final word for me."

Brant softened at the gentle chastisement. Nico was right. He was getting too into his head again. Dating as a gay man who was former military wasn't exactly easy waters to navigate. He decided to think further on it and changed the subject.

"So, what about you? Do you have your eye on anyone lately?" Brant asked, deflecting back to Nico.

Now it was Nico's turn to look abashed. He stared at Gus, who was trying vainly to get a kitchen drawer open with his front claw. There was a special new lock in this one, as it contained the cheese puffs that Gus liked so much.

"Well, yeah, there is a woman who's been coming to the gardens on a few of the school trips. She's a teacher. She's kind and funny. She's looked at me a couple of times with this 'look', you know? But I still can't tell," Nico finished wistfully.

Brant was happy to have the conversation turn from him, but he was even happier to learn that something had been simmering for Nico.

"Is this the first person you've been interested in since you transitioned?" Brant asked gently.

"Yeah, it's not been something I've been comfortable pursuing before. Too many changes. But the timing feels right. Now I just gotta —" Nico trailed off.

Brant finished Nico's sentiment confidently, " — ask her out. And you will, when you are ready. I'm sure the work thing makes it tricky, too." Brant acknowledged.

"Yeah. I'll just send her the signs that I'm open to it. Best I can do for now," Nico walked over to pry Gus's claws from the drawer that xer had finally managed to open just as Koffe's heavy knock sounded at the door.

"Do you want to try to talk this afternoon after work about all these newcomers?" Brant asked Nico, opening the door to a harassed-looking Koffe who walked in and set his bags down. Nico gestured wordlessly at the drawer to Koffe about what needed to be replaced. Again.

Nico replied, "That sounds great."

Brant closed the door behind Koffe and patted him on the back. "I'll get him up to speed on the latest while I finish packing this order," Koffe looked wary and spoke in his characteristic rumble, "Somebody new?"

"Several somebodies, actually. The roller coaster continues, my friend. Pull up a seat and start frosting cupcakes, I'll tell you all about it."

"Ask him about Oded!" called Nico mischievously before dashing out.

Brant threw a hand towel across the room at the side door to the sound of Nico laughing down the driveway.

Chapter 9

The air was sweet with night-blooming jasmine flowers when Nico pulled into the driveway that evening. The crowds outside had started to disburse before dinnertime as the new security measures meant that it was harder for them to catch a glimpse of Gus. Nico felt a grim satisfaction at disappointing them. *Brant is starting to rub off on me*, he thought, shaking his head. Gus had been especially chaotic that day with Koffe. Xer ran back and forth across the basement, up and down the stairs, even bumping xer's head against the basement access door that led to the backyard. Gus ate double the usual helping of bird carcasses and supplements, and it took several bribes to keep xer from tearing apart every toy in the house. Nico wondered if it was the influx of new people that was causing all these energy bursts from Gus. As Koffe left, he gave Nico a quick squeeze on the shoulder with his massive hand. "Let me know how it goes, eh?" he rumbled in his distinct tone, but Nico could hear the exhaustion underneath it. "Get some rest, Koffe. And thanks, we will." He waved goodnight to his friend.

Nico finally managed to find a show on TV that Gus would sit calmly for. It was a queer pirate show about a dandy pirate and Blackbeard who become friends, then enemies, then lovers. Nico had never seen the show before and was enjoying it while journaling the day's events when Gus finally slowed down enough to lay on the couch. Well, Gus was on the couch, as xer took up most of the couch these days, so Nico was seated in the worn, comfortable armchair.

Brant came in from his delivery and flopped on the small corner he could fit in on the couch. Gus raised xer's head and licked Brant suddenly, causing him to laugh. Nico smiled indulgently.

"So, did you call everyone?" he prompted.

"Yep." Brant replied shortly.

"Is Oded coming?" Nico said, with a teasing lilt.

"All of them are coming," Brant stood suddenly. "I'm going to go start on some appetizers."

Nico called, "Make something vegetarian, just in case!"

Thirty minutes later, the door alert went off on Brant's phone just as he was putting the finishing touches on a beautiful plate of mozzarella and tomato crostini, a delicate basil leaf perched on top of each. The delicious smell of fresh pesto drifted in the air as a pot simmered on the stove nearby, filled with wide pasta noodles. The pungent green sauce made with basil, olive oil, and pine nuts was heaped into a large bowl. Plates and glasses had been set out buffet style, and a large pitcher of lemonade added a sharp citrus note to the air.

Brant was feeling a thrill of dread and excitement over this evening. He didn't know what the newcomers were like (one in particular) but for the first time in weeks, his stomach had stopped clenching over worrying about Gus. Xer was growing fast and evidently wanted these people here, so he was trying to trust in Gus. *"Trust in Gus," that could be our new slogan around here,* he thought, smiling inwardly at the idea.

Overall, he knew that they were yet another responsibility to keep track of and manage but at least they weren't threatening Gus, panicking, or trying to take the dragon, so he and Nico could both try to relax and socialize among adults. And if Brant was being honest with himself, he had a tiny thrill at the idea of meeting someone new. A love interest, he might even admit. *Naw, can't give Nico the satisfaction,* he smirked as he went to answer the door.

Standing in their driveway were all the same people from earlier that day, but there was a new person at the back. She was a petite older woman in her 60s, dressed smartly in a light brown silk blouse under a tailored cream linen jacket with a matching skirt that landed exactly at the knees. She was barely five feet tall, but she wore heavy, expensive jewelry that draped off her slender frame. She looked frail, but there was a serious don't-test-me vibe to her that Brant instantly admired. Her wild, brown curly hair was so freshly styled that it looked as if she had just left the salon. She locked eyes with Brant and with an irritated look, pushed past the surprised newcomers with 50 bracelets jangling, and tutted in a thick Italian accent before exclaiming, "I'm going to die of starvation before any of you invite me in. I need coffee," and that was how everyone gathered met Ms. Marguerita C. Scarpelli.

As soon as Ms. Marguerita plowed in through the side door, the others followed suit. Brant was just turning from shutting the door and blinds when he saw her standing stock-still as Gus jumped up to lick her face. Nico was straining to get Gus down without tearing her delicate suit and both Sylvester and Oded were helping him by holding each of Gus's claws as xer stood on xer's back legs, tongue lolling in pure delight. Ms. Marguerita was laughing but protesting at the same time, "Ahh! This one is so playful!" she said to Brant and Nico, then turned back to Gustopher dramatically, "Oh! You've got me!" she cried, extracting herself gently by backing up.

She took a deep breath of the smells wafting from the kitchen. "Ah," she said, a clear note of satisfaction in her voice as she eyed the spread, "someone who knows how to welcome strangers. With food." She went immediately to get a plate and set about loading it high. Brant and Nico raised eyebrows at each other. Brant mouthed silently, *Are you going to ask her?* and the eyebrows and shake-of-the-head reply from Nico, *Not me. You do it.* Brant shook his head in response, *No way.* Instead, they greeted everyone from the morning and gestured to gather around the table.

Once everyone had finished eating, Brant and Nico stood with Gus, who was chewing on a bird carcass in the corner near the front door and ignoring everyone completely. Ms. Marguerita was not taking her eyes off Gustopher, watching xer eat with open fascination.

Oded had glanced at Brant a few times over the meal, making Brant blush uncomfortably. Nico cleared his throat to rescue his friend.

"Everyone, thank you so much for coming back. We would all like to get to know you further, and talk a bit more about what we think is happening — "

Ms. Marguerita interrupted Nico. "What is happening is that your dragon here is gathering strength."

Nico looked at her curiously. "And what makes you say that Ms. — ?" he trailed off, prompting her.

"I believe you've been expecting me. I am the historian sent from the tribunal. My name is Marguerita C. Scarpelli; you may call me Ms. Marguerita," she said firmly. "I am here to ascertain if...Gus, is it? is in the right environment for xer's transformation."

Nico was startled at her use of Gus's pronoun without being prompted. Marguerita's eyes gleamed and she smiled with satisfaction again. "Oh, yes, I know all about their pronouns. I presume you are the one who's been getting the visions."

Now it was Brant whose mouth was hanging open. "Wow, Ms. Marguerita, you really know your stuff," he said in admiration. "Please, clue us in. We could use the information about the...transformation, did you say?"

He glanced around and found that everyone was just as intrigued. Was there anything as delectable as juicy news?

Nico and Brant both brought her a barstool to sit on, so she had a better vantage point of Gus. Brant took her seat at the table, next to Oded. Oded's mouth crinkled a little at the corner but said nothing. Brant looked down and was studying his napkin avidly.

Nico was watching Gus, who seemed very content and was dozing softly now. Ms. Marguerita began, "I do work with your tribunal sometimes, yes. There are often cases where lack of information can cost human lives — something the magical community is determined to avoid — so it's been my mission to learn as much as I can about our magical kin so that our coexistence can be as peaceful as possible."

"Are you reporting back to the tribunal on what you see and learn?" Brant asked shrewdly.

"Ah, okay. You are ex-militia, yes? It would make sense that this is your question. The answer is, somewhat," She pointed a finger at Brant, and he blanched a little under her sharp gaze. "I tell them what is *vital only,* and more importantly, I report it to both human and magickind equally. I am considered an impartial judge who is here to determine what is critical for each species to know."

"Is Gus in danger?" Nico questioned softly. Ms. Marguerita turned her sharp gaze to Nico and studied him quietly. She nodded to herself a few times and said, "No. If anything, all of you and Gus are safer now than you've ever been in your lives," she had a rueful smile. "Even if the next few months will be a strain."

Nico was deeply relieved to hear this, even if it was from a stranger. Gus was so still and relaxed in the presence of everyone that he took this as a good sign. "You were speaking about transformation?" Nico offered.

"This is not your dragon's full size. Xer will reach the size of an African bush elephant by the time xer has completed the process."

A silence fell as everyone in the room swiveled to look at the large dog-sized dragon snoring peacefully in the corner and tried to picture an elephant there. Brant's face had turned completely white. Oded reached out and took Brant's hand, which he didn't even register. Oded was holding his hand comfortingly, as Brant was making some coughing, gasping sounds. Nico was taking this news slightly better, but only slightly. He kept picturing the amount of food they would need. His mind was boggled at the idea and was persistently short-circuiting. Sylvester took pity on Nico and came over to pat him on the back. Quietly he murmured, "It's going to be okay, man."

Finally, Nico spoke just as Brant took a calming breath with a shudder. "Okay, so now I see the full picture. Ms. Marguerita, how do you know all of this?"

She snorted a little, saying, "You haven't even begun to know the full picture, but that's why I'm here, young man. Please, listen, and don't interrupt."

Ms. Marguerita settled a little in her seat before continuing, "I've been a mythical creature folklorist and historian my whole life. I had already been studying the lore of magical creatures for 26 years — especially dragons — when the fae came out last year. I've been expecting a reunion of the species for some time, in truth. The spaces where fae can live have been growing smaller and smaller for too many years. They periodically come out and interact with humans to reestablish their...habitats, for lack of a better word."

Nico knew he couldn't process everything at once, his mind was spinning too rapidly. He went to the living room to grab his journal. He brought it back and turned to a new page to take notes.

"Excellent," Ms. Marguerita said, sounding almost relaxed. "We have a chronicler here. Show me," she commanded, and Nico handed her the journal. Brant was still trying to come out of shock. Oded had taken to patting him on the back and shoving some tea closer to his hand. Nico could hear Brant muttering, "The cheese puffs alone are going to cost a fortune."

As she studied the journal, she said almost offhand to Nico, "Are the visions of you next to Gus, or inside?"

"It's as if I'm the one experiencing it," he said sadly, remembering the snowy landscape. "Is that how you know their pronouns?"

Ms. Marguerita stiffened slightly. "We are getting off-topic," she said briskly. "I will need to speak to you both privately, but I presume you want to meet with these people first?"

Brant had finally snapped his attention back and turned to look at Oded, who had pulled closer. Brant smiled at the trust and affection there and then seemed to remember himself.

He stood and said, "Okay, so now that *that* new information has come to light, I would love the distraction of hearing what you all talked about today."

Koker stood and addressed Brant, though his eyes kept darting to Gustopher.

I've decided to move to Multnomah. I'm bringing my accounting practice here. I understand that some of what I'm feeling is under the influence of Gus," he broke off, looking at the dragon with open affection, " but I truly think that I was brought here for a reason, and I also feel in my heart that this is the right change for where I am at." He smiled almost forlornly and said as an afterthought, "I've spent too much of my life waiting for something to happen. It's time to stop waiting and start living."

Koker sat back down, and Gus came over to rest xer's head on Koker's lap, letting out a satisfied chuff.

Laszlo stood next, following Koker's example. They cleared their throat and said, "I'm a carpenter by trade. I can always find work. I'm also moving to Multnomah. I don't have any ties to Utah, so I can move here pretty easily," they glanced around the kitchen appraisingly. "You've had some great work done in here. I could help with reinforcements outside, if you'd like." They looked to Brant, and Brant nodded in agreement. Laszlo sat back down and reached out to scratch behind Gus's ear, still with xer's eyes closed in contentment, resting on Koker's lap.

Sylvester stood next. " I contacted some folks back in Seattle, and they can handle things for a few months while I figure out what all this is," he gestured vaguely at the house, encompassing the whole scene. Nico felt a stab of sympathy. He knew all too well how one pivotal event can change your life. It was hard to get your bearings in a rapidly changing environment. He and Brant shared a knowing look, remembering that fateful day that everything had changed for them, too.

Sylvester finished by saying, "But you've got me for a few months, so I'd like to help where I can." He sat back down and looked at Nico, nodding agreeably. Nico returned the nod.

Oded didn't stand, but instead, surveyed the other strangers. He frowned slightly, then turned to Brant. "So what exactly are we supposed to do here? Even if I move, what am I doing?" He gave a snort of self-depreciating laughter. "I'm a musician, not a fighter. If I need to brawl someone in the street, I'm not your guy."

Brant admired the long view that Oded was taking and stifled a smile at how his mind worked. Now was not the time to make googly eyes at the handsome man who was currently lounging in his dining room chair.

"An excellent question. We are going to be working out a plan very soon — probably with Ms. Marguerita's help — to figure out our next steps concerning some pressures that have been coming at us, basically, from all directions. I'm sure you all noticed the crowd outside this morning, right? Believe it or not, that's one of many issues going on right now. The magical tribunal's demands are our most pressing concern," Brant said, trying not to linger on Oded's eyes while everyone was watching him. He glanced at Nico, who was grinning a little *too* knowingly.

"I mean, I have decided to move here as well," Oded continued mischievously, "I was just wondering what I can bring to the group. I don't want to be useless. As a classical musician, it's hard to justify me taking up space," he said wryly, but Nico could tell he was joking. Cluelessly, Brant took the bait.

"What are you talking about? The arts are just as important as finance, or construction, or community outreach. I'll bet your music has changed more lives than you realize," Brant said, fiercely.

Oded grinned at how quickly Brant began defending his vocation. Nico turned and faced the living room, his shoulders shaking with laughter that Brant was falling for this man before his eyes.

Nico took a deep, steadying breath and was turning back just as Oded said, beaming, "Thank you for saying that. I hope every day that that's true as well. It will be a little bit tricky with my touring schedule starting up this summer, but I think I can swing it. I'm in temporary housing right now anyway, because I'm about to hit the road. I'm collaborating with a bunch of other musicians."

Brant blushed again, clearly pleased. He stood and addressed everyone. "Okay, that's settled then. Everyone is going to be new residents of Multonmah. May I be the first to welcome each of you. Nico, any follow-up?"

Nico had collected himself and looked around. "I'm sure we'll have questions for you all later, but right now, we need to talk to Ms. Marguerita in private. It's going to be a long session, and I don't know how much of this will interest you. How about we get in touch with you in the next few days, and let you coordinate the logistics?" Everyone nodded in agreement.

Ms. Marguerita spoke brusquely, "Since it's getting late, I think we should postpone until tomorrow. I would prefer to consult some texts first, anyway. I will contact you in the morning and we can meet then. Set aside several hours and invite whomever you want, as long as they practice discretion," she warned, and she left as abruptly as she had arrived.

Gus stood by the side door and nuzzled the hands of everyone who filed out to leave, but as Oded was the last person to move towards the door, xer jumped up on Oded's chest, nearly knocking the musician over.

"Gus! Be careful!" scolded Brant, who carefully extracted the claws from the front of Oded's shirt. He patted the musician's chest unnecessarily, smoothing the invisible wrinkles and feeling his strong muscles beneath it in appreciation. He glanced at Oded, who was smiling back at him, and Brant snatched his hand away as if he'd been burned.

"Sorry about that. I really should've asked first."

Oded's gaze softened. "I appreciate that." He paused briefly and looked at Brant meaningfully. "And the answer is, yes."

Brant looked both relieved and confused. "Yes, to what?" he asked, a little dash of hope evident in his voice.

Oded turned to the door and walked out. Over his shoulder, he said, "Just in general. The answer, when it comes to you, is yes." His tone was soft but sure. He had said it low enough that only Brant could hear it. It gave him a shiver of excitement down his spine and warmed his chest. He didn't trust himself to speak, so he just shut the door, softly.

He watched Oded walk down the driveway, basking in the glow of this feeling of being what, horny? infatuated? It had been so long since he'd had a romantic reaction to someone, not to mention to have had it reciprocated. He'd almost started to believe it was never going to happen for him, to find love.

Wait, was this about love? Or was it just hormones? Brant's thoughts were storming, and he turned back to Nico and Gus.

Nico had moved to the living room with Gus and pulled out his journal to scribble down his questions for Ms.

Marguerita. But as Brant flopped into a chair, he looked up. Nico's smile was gentle, his eyes shining with happiness.

"Big day." was all he said.

"Big day," Brant agreed. "Big damn day."

CHAPTER 10

Late April

Over the next few days, Brant and Nico collected a list of questions and concerns for Ms. Marguerita and organized them. The list was sectioned into three categories: what was crucial for them to know to face the tribunal, what they would be willing to share with perceived allies and non-allies, and what they wanted to keep private for the time being. For instance, Gus's new ability to vanish into thin air. The strange sonic pulse that xer had sent out after xer's unconsciousness was also something they needed to keep under wraps, especially since the military was sniffing around.

Knowing that they had an advocate to work with who they didn't have to educate was a great comfort to Nico, especially. There was no having to catch her up to speed, no adjustment period for her to accept or to wrap her mind around the controversy of Gus brewing just outside their door. Mysteriously, she seemed to know a bit already about some of the fantastical things Gus could do. Even the fact that she was aligned with the tribunal didn't bother Nico as much as it did Brant, who was prone to think of the worst-case scenario. Nico respected that about him, but also felt that it was vital that Ms. Marguerita could shed some light on the aspects of

Gus that they both desperately wanted to understand. Why was he getting these visions and not Brant? What did they mean? What did she know about dragon history and customs? Was there something that they could be providing xer to make Gus's life better, something that would get the tribunal off their back? And probably the most puzzling question of all, how *and why* did Gus originally go from xer's full size as a dragon to the size of a small gargoyle?

Nico had all these thoughts on his mind while he was at work on a gorgeous day in late April and it caused so much distraction that Bisan, the teacher he had just opened up to Brant about, came over to him and nudged him before he even noticed she was there. The dappled sunlight through the trees cast across her curly brown hair and brought out the golden flecks in her eyes. She moved slowly through the gardens, touching plants with real affection, caressing their leaves with a light touch. Her laugh was lovely and musical whenever she observed the children, and it gave Nico such a happy, home-like feeling every time he heard it. Embarrassed, he looked down at his feet, shuffling them slightly. He wanted so badly to ask her out but still couldn't be sure if the vibe was mutual. After his recent conversation with Brant when he talked about his concerns, he felt a little bit braver today. He decided to send her a clear sign and see how the response was.

"So, how are the kids behaving?" Nico said, smiling at her warm expression as she watched the students. She shrugged a little and glanced back at the little cluster of kids who were almost touching their noses to the surface of the water, watching the koi fish in the pond. It was always a main attraction. "One of them got a bloody nose, but it was easy enough to clean up. They love coming here," she paused slightly. "We all do," she said softly, looking at Nico for a moment longer than she had to. Nico cleared his throat and glanced at the group, making sure they weren't getting too close to the water. He looked back at Bisan and stood a little straighter. He ignored his lurching stomach and started, "You know, there's a great outdoor kids program I looked up recently at Oaks Bottom Wildlife Refuge. They host a special week to study amphibians. I could meet you there with a group one day. You know, to keep you company. Maybe help identify some plants."

Bisan's smile was positively radiant.

"You looked up a program for my kids?" she said simply.

"Yes," said Nico, hesitantly.

"And you want to *keep me company*," her emphasis on the phrase was clear, "and show me some plants?"

Nico could see the playful happiness on her face, and his heart melted at the relief. He tried to keep his cool and failed utterly by blurting out, "Well, show the kids some plants. You know, it's for the children."

"Right, right," she said, openly laughing now, "the poor children. Forced to go on yet another outing until I could get my favorite bonsai gardener to finally ask me to... study some plants," she finished with a wink. Nico's heart nearly exploded with the euphoria.

"Well, since you did all this research, I wouldn't want it to go to waste. It's a date," she said firmly. She reached out and patted Nico on the shoulder. "I should get back, though. Should we exchange numbers?" she asked, already pulling out her mobile phone and handing it to Nico with no small amount of triumph.

Nico ducked his head a little, putting his number into her contacts. She promptly sent him a message with a small leaf and a lizard. He looked up to smile at her again, but she had already hurried back to the group of students. Watching her gave Nico a trailing ribbon of happiness he had not felt in years. He tucked that feeling close to his heart for the rest of the day

As Nico was pulling into the driveway, he spotted Ms. Marguerita's car. He hurried up to the new fence that shielded the view of who was at the side door from the prying eyes of the ever-present crowd on the sidewalk. They were still holding their signs of both encouragement and damnation. Their stubborn desire to camp out on their street had caused a real strain on the neighborhood, but Nico couldn't focus on that now. He unlatched the fence and walked up to his door, hearing the scramble and thunder of claws across the floor from Gus. He winced briefly, wondering how Brant was taking the damage to his grandmother's house. He made a mental note to check in with his friend.

As Nico braced himself for impact, he could see Ms. Marguerita and Brant in the kitchen, sharing a laugh with a delicious dessert of Brant's halfway to her mouth. She closed her eyes in clear luxury, and Brant risked a quick wink and a nod to Nico as he came in. Ms. Marguerita was susceptible to the charms of Brant's kitchen talents. It was Brant's own form of magic, really. Her happy sigh was sign enough for Nico that they were off to a good start.

She finished the treat in a few short bites, brushed her hands on a napkin, and dabbed delicately at her lipstick. She was dressed immaculately again, this time in a turquoise and pink pantsuit. Her jewelry made faint tinkling sounds as she moved. She waved at both men to sit in the living room, and everyone settled into the space. Nico noticed that there was an extraordinarily high pile of mail on the dining room table; there were hundreds of letters there. He gestured to Brant silently with a nod of his head and a raised eyebrow, but Brant just shook his head, no, and mouthed, *I'll explain later.*

Nico shrugged, pulled out his journal, and settled in the easy chair.

Ms. Marguerita had sat neatly on the couch. She had one ankle tucked behind the other. Gus sat down with her and was being uncommonly gentle like the last time she was here, which Nico was thankful for.

Brant took the spare armchair and had settled in with a beer nearby. He had brought Nico a lemonade without prompting, and Nico gave him a nod of gratitude in return.

Ms. Marguerita began, "All right. Settle down and listen closely. I have many things to share, and you will need your wits." She cleared her throat importantly.

"The historical records about dragons were passed down from thousands of years of oral tradition, so even the best approximation we have are fragments. But I've dedicated my life to putting those fragments together, so I will start at the beginning.

From what we can tell, for a very, very long time, humans lived in a symbiotic relationship with wolves, bears, and yes, dragons. We have stories of relationships of apex predators and human cooperation in every continent dating back as far as human records go. There was a clear advantage for all the species to cooperate during times of drought, famine, or natural disasters such as floods, fire, volcanic eruption, earthquakes, tornadoes; all of it. The bears, wolves, and dragons could hunt in sparse terrain with their sense of smell, scout ahead over long distances faster than humans, and survive better in harsher climates. And when times were plentiful for humans, in turn, they would leave out offerings for the apex predators. Dragons especially, with the additional gift of flight, were useful to humans. But there was a singular way that dragons interacted with humans around communication that was different from the other predators."

Ms. Marguerita glanced at Nico briefly, a flash of a complicated emotion on her face that Nico couldn't read. Brant watched this exchange, puzzled. He urged her, "You were talking about how they communicate? Does this have to do with Nico's visions?"

Ms. Marguerita nodded solemnly. "Yes, but it goes deeper than that. Elders of human tribes — especially the women — were revered for their emotional connection to dragons. The dragons held a special place of honor because of their connection to our ancestral elders.

"Humans survived as long as we did largely due to all of these species, but it was dragons in particular that assisted with maintaining tribal wisdom, developing our history and legacy, and our finding acceptance of all kinds of humans that were developing across the globe. They facilitated interpersonal tribal disputes; they mediated over territory squabbles. They brought out the strongest of our talents," Ms. Marguerita paused briefly to take a drink of water. She seemed to be wrestling internally with what to say next. Brant and Nico waited anxiously, the desire to learn more plain on their faces. Gus had appeared to be napping at the start of the discussion but now opened one eye to study Ms. Marguerita briefly.

"This next bit of information is not public knowledge, even in the historical records. Let's just say I have confirmed this information unequivocally. The tribunal may not like that I'm sharing this, but if you are already receiving the visions, there's truly no stopping what is about to happen next," she took a deep breath, stroking Gustopher's ear lightly. Gus closed xer's eye in happy contentment.

"Each dragon has an affinity innate to them. Some dragon's affinity is rooted in something external, like a gift for music or a talent for architecture. Other dragons have an affinity that is more mercurial, such as diplomacy, or certain personality traits. Whatever that dragon's affinity is, it both draws that element out of the individuals around them — no matter the species — as well as attracts that talent closer to them. The older the dragon, the stronger the affinity. Think of it like a magnet or an amplifier effect. I suspect Gus's affinity is like that. What was the first thing you noticed about xer in this regard?"

Nico and Brant looked at each other thoughtfully. Brant spoke finally, saying, "Well, it was evident that Gus was drawing men closer to xer. There was a really strong protection vibe that kept happening. We thought it was because xer was so little and cute," he smiled to himself, remembering how chubby Gus was. Almost to himself, he said, "The ears were irresistible!"

Nico's face crooked into a smile as he glanced at the claw print art on the wall, memorialized in clay.

Brant's face fell into a puzzled expression, and he looked up at Ms. Marguerita with dawning realization. "Our friend Remi told us something right before he left. He said that Gus attracted good men. Do you think that is Gus's affinity?"

Ms. Marguerita stared at Brant, but her gaze had softened, and she was deep in thought. "It could be. It's hard to say. That is an affinity that's hard to test without more time. Only as Gus gets bigger and xer's powers grow to full maturity again will we know for sure. You will both need to be ready for that day, which is coming very soon. The tribunal is aware of dragon affinity, but without an effective way to communicate directly, the tribunal is reticent to make contact with Gus on xer's own. Dragons are extremely private creatures about their culture, their history, their mating, and reproduction. We cannot communicate with them; they have to choose to open up to us humans. And they are protective of those they perceive as their friends or family. Only the most revered ancestral elders were allowed to know the smallest details about them. And then there was the Great Severing, as we historians call it."

"What is that?" Nico said, anxiously.

Ms. Marguerita spoke softly now, almost as if she didn't want to hurt Gus's feelings. But xer continued sleeping peacefully, letting out the occasional chuff of content.

"It's just what we call it. We can tell from the records that there was a time of great collaboration, but then, something happened that severed the ties, and the dragons just...disappeared. The humans began to be more isolating, more exclusionary away from those other apex predators and even began shunning other humans who were different, who were easily identifiable as 'other.' This could be a physical difference or a behavioral one. They began to persecute these 'others.' They stopped leaving offerings at the crossroads and rejected the bears entirely. The wolves broke into two factions; ones who remained wild and those who chose to stay with humans, to try and teach them the value of unconditional love." Ms. Marguerita's voice had taken on an edge of grief and anger. She was struggling to keep her composure as she turned to Nico. Nico's eyes held compassion and the same grief.

"They burned the others, didn't they?" he whispered, barely able to get the words out. He could still smell the rancid air from that vision, so many weeks ago. Nico coughed and covered his face.

"Yes," she said, her voice breaking. "And worse," she said harshly. She stood suddenly, pacing back and forth in the living room. Brant and Nico took the moment to compose themselves, as they had both teared up at the idea of how heartbreaking the Great Severing must have been for Gustopher's kind.

Ms. Marguerita had walked over to the kitchen to help herself to another of Brant's confections for comfort. She took a bite and sighed. As she sat back down, she looked sternly at Brant and said with her usual sharp voice, "Young man, these are excellent. I need the recipe."

The moment allowed them all to shift the mood, and Nico was grateful for the change of subject. But Brant just flashed her his most disarming smile and said, "Not a chance. You can't bully me for that."

"Watch me." Ms. Marguerita retorted, but there was no bite to it.

"But wait," said Nico, "what about how Gus got from really big to small? And how did xer turn into a gargoyle?"

Ms. Marguerita faced Nico and replied sadly, "I wish I could tell you. I am sworn by the tribunal not to reveal that particular bit of information," she held a tight, private smile at the corners of her mouth. Pausing deliberately, she leaned into Nico's ear and said, "But I suspect you will know soon enough."

"No fair! I want to know, too." Brant protested. Ms. Marguerita waved a dismissive hand at Brant. She retorted, "That's what you get for not sharing your recipe."

Brant laughed softly in return, shaking his head. She continued,

"We need to discuss the town hall. I want to make sure you are aware of what's involved." Ms. Marguerita was back to her brisk demeanor.

"'Town hall' is a bit of a misnomer for humans. We will not be in a building, a recreational center, a church, or the like. It's more of a seasonal gathering to settle disputes, raise concerns, and form alliances. It coincides with the midnight market which brings tremendous trade for your region. The news of the dragon has already been buzzing for weeks amongst magickind. The tribunal feels the pressure to evaluate what to do next and the best steps for both worlds." Ms. Marguerita paused to let Nico catch up, as he was scribbling frantically in his notebook.

"I doubt I need to tell you how important this is. Magical communities all over the world are watching this event with great interest," she pointed a finger accusingly at Brant, who blanched but straightened up at the attention, "so keep your eyes open for any mischief-makers, human or otherwise, that seem to be from out of town or are trying to stir up trouble."

"Understood," Brant replied smartly. He resisted the urge to give Ms. Marguerita a salute, but he yearned to do it, for old time's sake. Ms. Marguerita reminded him of his military superiors, and he couldn't help but respond to that authority. *Well, at least one I respect*, he thought bitterly of the lieutenant colonel.

Nico was still taking copious notes, but popped his head up to ask, "What about the proceeding itself?"

"Yes, I'm getting to that. First, you must arrange transport of Gus to the town hall. Xer must be brought separately from you so that xer's persuasive magic over you has a chance to dissipate before the assessment. Second, you *must* be on time. This is of paramount importance. You risk the highest and deepest possible insult if you are late. The timing is critical, and there must be nothing left to chance. Be there a full half-day early if you must.

Lastly, unless I tell you to do so, do not speak. I will speak on the benefits and risks of having Gus in this region. Humans are typically not versed in the customs of a magical tribunal. It's my understanding that you — " she glanced at Brant with something like begrudging admiration, "— did tolerably well when the tribunal showed up, but this will be a longer encounter, and you are very likely to say something disastrous and ruin your chances," Ms. Marguerita huffed slightly to herself at the thought. Gus shifted slightly in his sleep, putting his back leg gently next to hers.

"I'm so confused. Is it like a human court? Who is the other attorney?" Nico said, looking flustered.

"You do not 'make your case', young man." Ms. Marguerita said shortly, but there was a sympathetic tone underneath.

"I am the ambassador for both species. I will present the benefits and risks and they will make their judgment. Your job is to show up and receive the decision with Gus present. As far as the tribunal is concerned, you've already misstepped by not turning Gus over immediately when xer was found, so now, you must face the magical authority in this area for their wisdom." Brant began to protest, but Ms. Marguerita raised one finger and Brant immediately quieted. Such was the power of a crotchety old Italian.

"Your falsified documents might work in the human world, but not among magickind," she admonished.

Nico puzzled aloud, "If the tribunal knew about Gus when Rubra was looking for xer after the abduction, why didn't they come after Rubra?"

Ms. Marguerita gave an impatient sigh. "The timing of everything went sideways from the start. And there are enemies and alliances changing every season around here. Who can say if you were lucky, foolish, or both up until now?" she replied philosophically, raising her joined fingers in the classic Italian gesture, wiggling her wrist slightly. She looked at Nico before she said, "May I continue?" but it held all the sweetness of a disturbed viper. Brant shook with repressed laughter, his lips pressed together while he pretended to rub his eyes.

Without waiting for an answer, Ms. Marguerita continued. "The judgment will go one of three ways: Gus will be allowed to stay with you; Gus will be moved to a magical family; or xer will be released into the wild. Only in the first scenario will you both be allowed to see xer." Before she could continue, Gus sat up and climbed off the couch.

Gus pulled xerself to full height and lowered xer's head down to stare directly at Ms. Marguerita, still seated. She visibly drew back at Gus's gaze but did not break eye contact. Nico and Brant held their breath. They had never seen Gus look so...aggressive. Gus let out the same deep rumble xer had made at the casino when confronting Viscidius Rubra. Brant and Nico were both rising to de-escalate the growing discomfort. Brant approached Gus gently, placing a hand on top of xer's shoulder, saying softly, "Easy now, little dude. She isn't the enemy here," while Nico also stood close to Ms. Marguerita, attempting to block Gus's view of her.

Slowly, Gus raised xer's head imperiously, turned very deliberately, and walked out of the room, their claws thudding the floor. The air was thick with an ominous and vague threat that was stubborn to dissipate. All three humans let out ragged breaths of relief.

Ms. Marguerita stood calmly and smoothed her clothes, but Nico could see her hands were trembling. She curled her fingers around her portfolio and walked purposefully towards the side door. She turned and addressed both men: "I wish it were only up to Gustopher, but sadly, it is not. The balance between magickind and humans is precarious right now. We will see what the future holds."

And with that dreadful little tidbit, she left.

CHAPTER 11

First Week of May

After Ms. Marguerita's visit, Brant and Nico started to dread the upcoming town hall more acutely. It didn't help that the residents of the surrounding blocks had finally lost their patience over the growing crowds congesting their normally tranquil street. The neighbors had taken their complaints straight to the City, and Mayor Flint had sent a letter requesting them to set up a meeting at his office. As much as Nico and Brant wanted to meet the mayor, truthfully, their hands were full with Gus and the onlookers outside were the least of their problems. The mayor's letter lay on top of the growing pile of mail on the dining room table.

The letters that Nico had spotted were from people all over the country. Once word had spread from the horrible radio program that there was a real-life dragon right in the center of Multnomah, the public's imagination had run wild with the possibilities. Nico and Brant tried to make the best of a bad situation somewhat by reading the positive letters aloud to Gus and each other. Brant's hands were usually full of yarn as his fingers flashed, needles clacking with unspoken frustration. By far, the best were from little kids, with their loose, loopy writing and misspelled letters. Some of them treated Gus as if xer had godlike powers, some wrote as if xer were a sibling and they were sharing secrets.

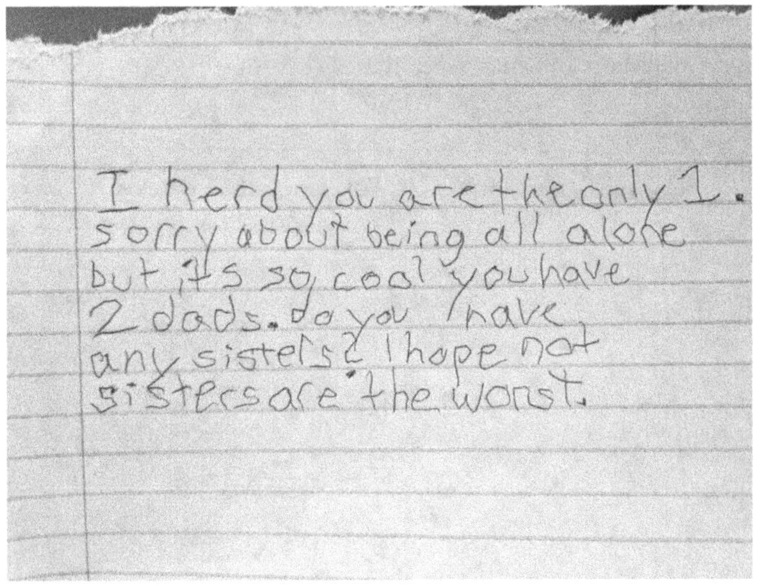

These questions made Brant and Nico very thoughtful. Gus turned away more than once when an innocent question seemed to strike a nerve. Xer had lost the joy xer had had when the new strangers had arrived and was prone to sulking in the basement, despite his family's attempts to draw xer to communicate or play as a group. Even the visions had stopped happening, and Nico felt an emptiness in their absence, which was not a sentiment he expected to feel even a few weeks ago.

Lieutenant-Colonel Hayworth had come by again, just as blustery and domineering as the first time, and Brant closed the door firmly in his face, again. The days ticked by relentlessly towards June 21st.

On May 2nd, just a week after Ms. Marguerita had left, Nico, Brant, Koffe, and Paula were all together in the backyard behind the reinforced fence enjoying the gentle breeze and fading sunset over a shared dinner. The basement access door had been cleared off and thrown open so that Gus could hear them from xer's spot in the basement, even though Gus was acting sullen.

They were all attempting to coax Gus outside, and xer's dads suspected that with the growth spurts and mood swings, they might have a teenage dragon on their hands, rather than an overgrown toddler. Gus had become significantly less gangly even in just a few weeks. Xer's movements were more graceful, and the claws and horns had lengthened to some degree. The scales had become harder but had a pearlescent evergreen sheen to them that caught the light beautifully.

They were all enjoying a low conversation about current events in their lives when Nico heard a familiar voice call his name from the carport. He felt a shock of recognition and dread, turning to Brant and motioning for quiet. Koffe and Paula were instantly on their feet, but Nico only shook his head in disbelief.

It couldn't be...but was it? Nico heard the voice call his name again, a lump forming in his throat. He stood and walked over to the gate, peering on his tiptoes. Staring back at him was his father's face.

Brant was enjoying the reprieve in the mild spring air with his friends and Nico. It had been a long time since he'd taken an evening for himself. He had recently been able to hire some part-time help to assist with the running of the cookie truck, and it was a welcome relief to turn over even just a couple of tasks from the thousands of decisions he made every day to someone else, even if it was the lower-priority ones. It was a trial run with having staff, but it was already providing relief to the household, given the upcoming town hall that was weighing on his mind. He was just beginning to relax and finally let his shoulders drop when he could sense Nico's body tense next to him as they both heard a faint call near the side of the house.

It was not unusual to hear neighborhood noises at this time of year. The kids often played in the street, the neighbors were out puttering around in their yards, and the tinkerers had their garage doors open, making all the hectic happy noises of a creative project punctuated by colorful language, of course. He could even smell the distinct aromas coming from someone's barbeque, the light, musical sound of glasses being toasted accompanying the sounds of relaxed laughter. So Brant was especially surprised to turn and see Nico's mouth drop open, astonished. Before he could ask about the voice, Nico had moved quickly to the fence gate, peering over it to see who was there. It couldn't have been one of the public, since Nico seemed to recognize the voice.

Brant leaned a little in his seat, craning to get a look at the person Nico was so fixated on. He heard Nico's urgent tone and was just getting concerned when Nico opened the fence gate and gestured for the stranger to come in.

Brant absorbed the proud stance of an older Latino man with greying temples and a sharp gaze. He stood about 5'9 and favored a limp in his right leg. He examined the backyard and the inhabitants with a cautious and closed look but did glance at Nico a few times as if he hadn't seen him in a long while.

Nico looked extremely uncomfortable. His eyes were downcast, only glancing at the open basement door once. He gestured wordlessly to a chair for the stranger, and the man sat down with formality. Brant, Koffe, and Paula all looked up expectantly at Nico, waiting for an introduction, but Nico only looked down, deep in thought. After a moment, he seemed to come to a decision when he raised his eyes, looked at the stranger, and said, "Welcome, Papa. These are my friends, Koffe and Paula. And this is my best friend and roommate, Brant. Everyone, this is *mi padre*, my father, Vico."

Vico nodded at each one in turn in a solemn but respectful nod. His eyes studied Brant for a few moments, but he said nothing. He turned back to Nico and said, "Your mother wants to know why we haven't heard from you about Mother's Day. Are you coming home to celebrate?" His tone was a bit clipped, and Brant could hear the hurt under the abrupt question. "Your family misses you, *mija*."

What was discomfort before in Nico's face turned to anger in a flash. Nico's fists balled tightly, and he shifted his stance, taking a step away from where his father was seated.

"Mama could have called herself, Papa," Nico returned flatly, clear hostility in the statement. "Why are *you* here?"

Koffe and Paula stood awkwardly and quietly shuffled to a corner of the yard where they would be out of earshot. But Brant stayed firmly in his chair, determined to support his friend and defend him, as needed.

But before Vico could answer, Gus stalked, lightning-fast, up and out of the basement access stairs and was next to Vico in an instant. Xer was on all fours, wings spreading menacingly and fluttering almost lazily toward the man. It was as if Gus was sending out a warning and pointing it deliberately toward Vico. The message was plain, *Be careful.*

Father and son's faces both changed, but where Nico's was one of astonishment, Vico's was one of pure horror. He scrambled back, crawling out of the chair, all limbs and tangled legs as he bolted, trying to put some distance between the dragon and himself. Brant stood and put out a calming hand at Gus and the dragon had the cheek to wink at him briefly before settling into a docile seated position, tucking xer's wings in as if nothing had happened.

Vico was already at the fence gate, hand clutching his chest. Nico had followed his father to the fence and was speaking to him in a hushed tone. Brant couldn't make out what was being said but he could tell by the hand gestures and the cadence of Nico's voice that he was explaining about Gus. Brant caught fragments like "chose us," and, "needs our help," and "reactions just like this" but Vico kept shaking his head back and forth, clearly in denial of what was plainly in front of him.

Not the only thing he's in denial about, Brant thought sadly as he recalled that Nico's father had used the feminine version of 'child' when addressing Nico. He knew that Nico's family was still adjusting to him being trans, but he didn't realize it was this bad.

Brant tilted his head slightly to look down at Gus and said, "Did you draw Vico here with persuasion to force him to talk to Nico? Or did you draw him here just to prove to Nico you would protect him, or was it both?"

Gus's face had taken on a stoic, stern expression during the discussion across the yard but now he turned and looked up at Brant, breaking into xer's old goofy, toothy grin. "You picked that up from Remi, didn't you? Trying to charm us into forgetting how impossible you are." Brant sighed dramatically but also rested a hand on Gus's head, giving xer a scratch behind the soft, velvety ears.

He gestured for Koffe and Paula to come back and sit, and they all settled back in their seats. Vico had calmed somewhat, but his eyes kept darting over Nico's shoulder back to Gustopher.

Nico finally urged his dad through the gate, walking him out to his car. Brant watched Nico and felt a pang of sadness. He should bake up Nico's favorite dish to help comfort him tonight. Koffe and Paula had diplomatically changed the topic, giving Brant a moment to his thoughts. Gus had settled down next to Brant after father and son had left, but as Nico came back in the gate, his hand raking through his hair distractedly, Gus stood again. Nico walked over and gave a weary smile to his friends.

Brant spoke low to Nico, "Hey man. What can I do?"

Nico smiled gratefully and said, "Can you dismantle a two-thousand-year-old patriarchal system?" Gus nodded at Nico, and Nico chuckled softly to himself. "I'll bet you could, *verdad.*"

Brant stood and clapped a hand on Nico's shoulder. "One heart at a time? Yes, yes, we can." He looked back at Koffe and Paula and saw they were listening now and smiling encouragingly up at Nico.

Koffe spoke first. "Families can be very resistant to change. It's good that you stood your ground. With a little help," he said, glancing over at Gustopher. Xer lifted a shoulder in a shrug of nonchalance, but xer's eyes were full of mischief.

Paula spoke next in a soft, supportive tone. "I can't imagine what it must be like to see Gus for the first time at this size and not as a baby — or, looking like one at least," she laughed easily. "We all know that Gus is relatively harmless, but I can see what all the fuss is about. We just have to help them to understand that Gus is not a threat." She paused slightly, looking at the overturned chair. "It *was* pretty funny, though." They all smiled briefly at the memory.

Nico grew serious again and said, smiling sadly, "I appreciate it, all of you. I need to go do some writing for a bit. Please, enjoy the evening. I need some time to process." He walked slowly to the side fence gate and started to raise the latch when he found that Gus was padding silently beside him. Gus barely had to get up on his hind claws to reach the latch. Gus and Nico walked back into the house together, and Brant watched them both, lost in thought.

Why did my dad come by today, of ALL days? I don't know how much longer I can bear my father's judgment and my new life. I can't keep living small enough to fit into his narrow view. He acts as if I'm the only one in our family who has broken tradition, but <u>he broke rules too</u>, when he married Mama. And what are we going to do with Gus as xer gets bigger? After the tribunal, what will happen even if Gus does come home with us? There's so many unknowns.

CHAPTER 12

Mid-May

The next few weeks were a riot of activity. Everywhere Nico turned the weather was astoundingly gorgeous. If Multnomah was known for being rain-drenched and soggy most of the year, it was all worth it for the unspeakable beauty of color in late spring bursting out as far as the eye could see. Trees were nearly groaning, stretching up with new shoots and bright flowers waving gently in the breeze. The wildlife was everywhere; Nico caught flashes out of the corner of his eye many times around the gardens and in his neighborhood. During the day it was birds, ground squirrels, mice, and insects. If he saw something at night in the backyard, it was raccoons and opossums. The nearby hooting of the owls was reassuring in a way he couldn't describe.

People were coming out of the woodwork in all directions; walking dogs, biking, joggers out running everywhere. Children and adults played together in the yards and at the public parks. Nico saw countless picnics, games such as badminton and Ultimate frisbee, and even heard the inspirational shouts of a diving instructor giving lessons at the local swimming pool. He watched as they gracefully arched up before tumbling into complicated knots, hitting the water with the smallest splash possible.

The dragon boat racers were already out on the river training for the fall race, practicing their speed. Their bodies surged forward as they pulled with all their might on the oars, their taunt muscles visible from half a mile away. The boat sped along the water like a thrown marble on a smooth hardwood floor, the force of the team's momentum working in unison. It looked as if the entire city was soaking up every bit of good days available.

Nico had chosen to express his budding desire to socialize by meeting up with Bisan last week and a group of her kids at a state park. The outing had gone so well that he felt confident about asking her out for a real coffee date, which was set up for the next week. He dreaded trying to figure out how to tell her about Gus, but he reasoned to himself, there was no sense in telling her in case the date didn't go well, right? He didn't like the idea of all the things that could go wrong, but if he'd learned anything in the last few weeks, it was that all of them were going to have to be a lot braver in facing their fears.

But despite all these glorious signs of spring and wanting to be braver, Nico still decided not to go to his family's Mother's Day celebration. It pained him that they were struggling to accept him, but for Gus's sake, he bore it as quietly as possible.

Nico had taken the most comfort and delight lately out of watching Brant corral the bewildered newcomers that had started to arrive every couple of days at the house's side door. Nico was amazed they hadn't worn down the doormat, there were so many. People of every kind of gender expression possible had appeared, scratching their heads in confusion. Brant tackled this change in his customary take-charge manner. He had an organizational system that would rival most event planners.

It was a late morning on Nico's day off, and he sneaked a sample of one of Brant's cooling breakfast breads. His genius baker friend had laid out a huge sample tray for a client who wanted to taste test before her bi-annual book sleepover. The client hosted a book-themed event at a small inn where everyone brought their favorite books, graphic novels, or audiobooks to listen to. While the inn had a dine-in restaurant, having savory and sweet breads on hand for nibbling was a perk that the client couldn't resist. The reputation of Bohunkus had spread quickly enough for her to want to secure Brant's sweets to impress her friends.

Brant had been commissioned for all kinds of jobs since his truck opened, and Nico was bursting with pride at how entrepreneurial his best friend had become. He watched Brant dust off his hands on his well-loved apron and walk to the side door, responding to the alert that someone had arrived. Nico listened as Brant gave his newly memorized speech to the latest batch of strangers who were drawn to Gus's expanding energy.

"All right, listen up. My name is Brant. We know why you are here, even if you don't. This is your welcome packet and I'm going to need each of you to fill out these clipboards and choose a lanyard before you ask a single question. Shouldn't take you more than 5 minutes. There are chairs in the carport, don't wander, and help yourself to coffee and tea in the large carafes to your left." He shut the door before remembering something and opened it again. "Oh, and I'll be back out in 10 minutes to talk further."

Nico snorted as he was taking a bite, and loose crumbs fell across the plate and bounced onto the counter. Brant raised an eyebrow but grinned back.

"I know it's a bit rude, but listen, we've already had five more people show up *today alone*, and they are coming from farther and farther away. We need a simple way to sort them and find out who intends to stay and who doesn't." He slid a blank form across to Nico. "I made some edits this morning; what do you think?"

Nico scanned the document he was already familiar with. He read through the new questions that stood out.

"How far did you travel to get to Multnomah?"

"What is your current occupation?

"What are your hobbies and passions?"

Nico paused and looked up at Brant. He deadpanned, "Gosh, how many do you think will make it through to the next round of interviews? Should we be offering a wellness package along with benefits and bonuses?"

Brant snorted huffily, "Well if you have a better system, I'm all ears. Just asking them about their address didn't seem to get much information. Last week, two people said they were moving here, no questions asked. So I made up these," he handed Nico a lanyard with something printed on both sides. Nico held up the plastic laminated card, one side reading "*NEW RESIDENT* "and the other saying "*JUST VISITING*" in capital letters.

"You can't be serious." Nico slapped the counter gently, letting out a full laugh at the absurdity.

"I can't keep track! Do you know how many people are out there? 12, Nico!" Brant sounded both exasperated and amused. "Who knows how many are going to be here by week's end? By the time we get to the town hall, for all I know, Gus's magic will pull these buds with us, and we'll have a squad of 500, or more," he said, shaking his head at the idea.

"Well, if we do end up with a whole squad of amazing folks that Gus has brought to us, why not see if they can help us?" Nico reasoned. Brant snapped his fingers in excitement at the idea, pointing at Nico. Brant followed the train of thought excitedly. "We do need extra eyes on the house to protect Gus, not to mention on the sidewalk nosey-nellies —"

Nico followed up, "— and we can't keep calling in Koffe and Paula, they've put their lives on hold for us for too long. And as long as the new people know who it's for and what it all entails, then I say we turn this into a recruitment drive." Nico smiled warmly at Brant, who was nodding, lost in thought. "I was messing around earlier, but it does make sense."

Nico followed Brant to the door to accompany him in welcoming the new batch of visitors but as he stepped onto the carport, standing behind where everyone was seated in camp chairs, was Vico, Nico's father.

"Papa. What are you doing here?" Nico blurted out. Vico's face was softer than the first time, and he surveyed the crowd of newcomers with something like respect. He gestured to Nico silently with a nod of the head, and Nico followed him hesitantly to stand at the gate leading to the backyard. Nico paused to hear Brant's speech, and Vico waited with him.

Brant watched the two men standing together. They looked so similar, it was plain as day that they were family, and yet they each had such different dispositions. Brant's face held a serious expression as he glanced at Nico, who gave him an encouraging nod. As Brant turned back to the gathered faces, he spoke up in his most drill-sergeanty tone, letting his voice carry: "All right, new recruits! You all now know why you are here, or you should, at any rate. If you've decided to stay here in town, take a lanyard and turn it facing out, the side that says, 'New Resident,' so I can keep track of who's decided so far. If you want to see what all the fuss is about, come back tonight at 7 pm and you can meet Gustopher."

He paused slightly, letting them all take that in. "If any of you can help right away with security, carpentry, or helping me in the kitchen, it would be much appreciated. If you are on the fence, feel free to explore your welcome packet which includes a list of all the others that have already taken jobs and houses and are here for the same reason you are. That will get you connected to the others and help you make up your mind." He gestured a few times at both the house and out the driveway.

"The workshop tonight will include a meeting with Gustopher —whose pronouns are xer/xers, by the way — and if you don't know what that is, you have time to look it up or talk amongst yourselves about it. We will fill you in on the current situation and what's brewing," he paused momentarily, trying to think if there was anything else. "Dismissed."

Everyone scrambled to rise and empty the carport, and Brant started folding up chairs, answering a few questions from stragglers with, "come tonight and you'll get all your answers there."

Nico and his father both walked through the gate to the backyard and Brant headed inside to get ready for the day.

Nico was standing with his father in the backyard, the last place they had been together. Vico couldn't help but glance at the locked basement access door where Gus was sleeping, a nervous expression crossing his face. He turned back to Nico and let out a deep breath.

"Nico, I did not mean to leave here so upset. It was a shock to see your..." Nico filled in firmly, "Dragon." Vico swallowed visibly but continued reluctantly, " — yes, dragon. So, are you sure he is not a *demonio*?"

Nico sighed inwardly. It was tiring to constantly correct strangers about Gus, and his father was no different.

"Gustopher is a dragon. A gender fluid dragon who does not subscribe to only 'he' or 'she.' We made that mistake ourselves at first, too," Nico smiled with humility, "but Gus goes by 'xer.'" He looked towards the house, basking in the love and support that had sheltered him within its walls.

Emboldened, he said, "Is that going to be a problem?" Nico looked at his father with a confidence Vico had not seen before.

Vico was relieved to hear that a *demonio* was not haunting his child. The last two weeks had had many sleepless nights of worry.

He looked at Nico and clapped his hand on his son's shoulders.

"No, *mijito*, that is what I came to talk to you about. I am sorry for the way I've been acting. Your mother has been trying to explain to me for months, and I didn't get it, *pero*...somehow, seeing you last week, here, at home somewhere else, made me realize something. You are a man now." Vico looked past his son's face briefly to where his hand rested on Nico's shoulder, feeling the muscles underneath. He patted his son a few times reassuringly.

"It's been an adjustment. But look at you! With a beard growing, now, eh? It looks good on you." Vico smiled just a little, and Nico relaxed his crossed arms. "Is Brant your..."

Vico struggled with the words, and Nico realized in horror that his dad was trying to ask about his love life. He barked out a laugh. Vico looked startled.

"No, Papa. Brant is my best friend, and he's into guys, but I like girls. Actually, I am dating a teacher."

Vico gave a victory shake of Nico's shoulder. "That's wonderful, *mijo,*" using the masculine form of the Spanish term for a second time. Nico's throat tightened with emotion. He didn't trust himself to speak so he said nothing.

His father spoke a little softer now. "I need to get going. I will talk with your *abuela.* I know you said you needed some space but...don't be a stranger. If you are not ready for Mother's Day this weekend, that's okay. But your mother misses you." Vico reached out and hugged his son. Nico closed his eyes tight, letting himself feel the closed part of his heart relax and open as wide as the spring season around him for the first time since he transitioned. He squeezed his eyes against the tears, opened them, and saw Brant with two thumbs up, grinning like a maniac from the kitchen window that overlooked the backyard. Nico tried not to laugh outright, but it was a struggle. He said, "*Adios,* Papa."

Vico waved as he left the backyard and walked off to his car. Moments later, Brant came bounding out of the house and rushed up to Nico.

"Oh. My. God! Has your dad finally come around? THIS IS HUGE!"

Brant was bouncing like a cartoon back and forth on the balls of his feet. He reminded Nico of a kid at an amusement park for the first time.

"Yeah. It is. He called me *hijo.*"

"What does that mean?" Brant asked, confused.

"It means we are okay. He said he was going to talk to my grandmother."

"Even better!" Brant's bouncing continued into the house. He was already pulling out food from the refrigerator, putting together a sandwich with lightning speed. "I'm going to make your favorite foods and tonight, we will get all these new recruits familiar with us! It's going to be great!" Brant shoo'd Nico out of the kitchen, so he went, laughing, to take a shower. He thought about his father, his mother, and his grandmother, and how much he'd missed them in the last year. If his mother and father were both accepting, his grandmother would come around. Nico started to hum a little song to himself and stopped to water one of his favorite plants on the bathroom counter before starting his day.

That evening, the house was gleaming inside and out for all the newcomers who were already crowding into the carport and yard. There were over 20 new faces and Brant scanned them, trying to recall the names from the multiple intake forms. They came from a wide range of occupations, lifestyles, and backgrounds.

There was Eddie Lili, a nonbinary Black person who worked in commercial construction. Eddie had already offered to work with Laszlo on fortifying the garage and to construct a front yard fence. Ke Huy Fukuhara, an eye doctor. A cheery man who bounced restlessly around the carport and backyard in circles. He was wearing all white, including a small white cap with no brim.

Then there was Terri, a transman magician from Las Vegas. Terri looked as if they had stepped straight through a portal from the 1970s, complete with a brown and orange polyester shirt unbuttoned to show off a hairy chest and gold chains, slicked back hair, and bell-bottom pants. Terri's New Jersey accent could be heard across the yard when he laughed.

Silver was a quiet Indian man in his 30s who worked as a utility company electrician by day but spent his free time creating open-source blueprints on the weekends for clockmakers.

A stunning young charmer in her 20s was a transwoman named Alex who had already made contact with Ms. Marguerita, as she was a historian of ancient Egypt. Alex had thick curly hair and bright hazel eyes.

Charles Stringfellow Cobbs, an older Black man in his 60s was an auto mechanic from Detroit. His hands and nails bore the embedded grease from working 40 years on old cars. Then there was Daddy Nyx, a professional dominatrix who was currently in a deep conversation with Sawyer, an elementary school teacher. Brant wondered briefly what subject matter they might possibly have in common.

The sunset streaked across the sky in pinks, blues, purples, and yellows. It could be seen at the edges of the temporary cover that blanketed the backyard's open skyline. Laszlo and Koffe had done a fine job of putting it up to help with privacy.

What had started a few weeks ago as a small gathering at the dining room table had evolved into hosting gatherings of 20 or more in the garage or carport a few times every week.

Regardless of the outcome of the town hall, they were going to need a solution to the growing influence of Gus, and soon.

Brant met Nico's eyes from across the yard. The area had been decked out with softly lit lanterns, rows of folding chairs, and a refreshment table. The planter boxes on wheels had been moved to the sides of the modest patio floor for ease of movement.

Nico was hovering at the table of refreshments, checking the covers on the meats, cheeses, vegetables, crackers, muffins, and cookies. He peeked inside the cooler at the blueberry lemonade and ginger-peach soda that Brant had whipped up. His friend was a genius at putting people at ease, focusing on the smallest detail.

Nico was feeling a bit overwhelmed at seeing how broad Gus's impact had become. He knew it in his mind, but it was another thing to have a whole crowd of strangers here, in his backyard, who followed nothing more than a gut feeling. He took a deep breath and unnecessarily straightened napkins that were already perfectly stacked.

Brant's voice called softly from behind him. "Hey. Are you ready? Don't worry, I'll do the introductions. Is that cool? I know you've had a big day already."

Nico nodded, grateful that his friend recognized how hard it would be to stand in front of strangers. Even ones that were inclined to like Gus. "I will go get Gus. I think xer is playing somewhere."

"Great. Take Paula with you," Brant called, already walking to stand at the front of the spot where the chairs had been assembled. Nico quickly made his way to the back, gesturing at Paula who was in conversation with Wali, a Pakistani male nurse from New York, to join him. Paula quickly excused herself and as they climbed the stairs to the side door, "What is it?" she asked, curious.

Nico had just started to say, "We are getting Gus — " when he heard a plaintive whine coming from just outside the kitchen. At first, Nico couldn't find where the sound was coming from. He looked near the kitchen sink on the floor, where Gus had recently taken to napping, because xer knew it planted xer firmly in the way, but there was nothing there. He scanned the living room; nothing.

Paula was stifling a laugh when Nico finally located the dragon. Gus was facing the kitchen from the top of the basement stairs, plushie bumblebee in xer's mouth, letting out a low whine-grumble because, as Nico examined closer and saw the trouble, Gus's entire back half was stuck in the doorframe. Like Winnie-the-Pooh, stuck in a window.

CHAPTER 13

Brant had welcomed everyone to the workshop and was waiting as patiently as he could when he heard the whine coming from inside the house. He gestured to Koffe to go see what the delay was and fielded a couple of questions.

"Yes, you had a question, Mr. — ?" he trailed, prompting the speaker to offer their name.

"My name is Hermengildo Garcia Angeles, Junior," a man said in a thick Spanish accent. Brant nodded encouragingly.

Hermengildo continued, "Yes, what is a 'Gustopher'? I know you explained on the flyer that we are here because of some magical thing, but I don't know what the thing is. Is it safe?"

Brant paused and answered. "Yes, Gustopher is a gender fluid dragon who will be out here any moment," *What was taking Koffe so long?* he thought, trying to count the minutes since Nico and Paula had gone inside. "As a matter of fact, let me go get xer. I will be right back. Talk amongst yourselves, please." He hurried to the back of the yard, almost sprinting into the house.

He found a strange scene before him. Koffe was bent over, his broad hands splayed on his thighs, silent sobs of laughter erupting every time he glanced in Gus's direction. Paula was also struggling to keep her composure as she tried to cautiously approach Gus from the side. Only Nico looked horrified; the clear embarrassment and social pressure flushed his face. Brant could see Nico's jaw was clenched as he took in the predicament. Nico was looking around frantically for anything that could help free the dragon from the opening.

Brant strode over to Gus and as he got closer, Gus went from whining to an outright growl. Brant reached for xer's front claw to see if he could start to pull, but he didn't even make contact before Gus *snapped xer's teeth* at Brant.

Brant stood abruptly. *Oh absolutely not, this little crumpet has never sassed me before and we are not starting today*, Brant thought firmly to himself. He had an entire yard of people waiting to meet this magnificent pain in his ass and he would be *damned* if he was going to allow back-talk at this point.

"*Gustopher. Caesar. Josephine.* You stop that *right now* and let us help you. We have a whole host of people who want to know why on this blessed Earth you have PULLED them here, and I'm not going to bandy about with you just because you feel silly about getting stuck in a doorway."

Brant turned to Nico.

"Go slide underneath Gus and push xer from the back," he said nonchalantly.

Nico looked horrified. "What?"

Brant explained as patiently as he could, though his insides were screaming, "Go underneath Gus and give xer a push with your shoulder from behind."

"Absolutely *not*."

"Why not?"

"Because I value my life and I want nothing to do with Gus's backside."

"Well, I can't do it."

"Why not?"

"I'm too big. You don't want both of us to get stuck, do you?"

"I'm not answering that," Nico huffed, crossing his arms.

An unfamiliar voice came from the side door. "You know," they said, "I can help you with that."

Everyone turned at once and saw the lanky frame of one of the people from the workshop. *Eddie,* Brant recalled suddenly. *Yes, Eddie works in construction, they can help,* Brant realized. There was a small crowd of people behind Eddie. Not everyone, but enough people from the backyard that the throng was beginning to press in. Laszlo also waved a helpful hand from the back of the crowd.

A few snickers came from the group, and Gus began growling again. Hastily, Brant said, "Yes, those of you *with experience,* come in and assist. The rest of you, please give some space for Gus as we work through this." Reluctantly, the larger cluster faded from the doorframe and Brant could hear the gate latch open as they drifted to the backyard. This was *not* the introduction Brant had hoped for, but it certainly was characteristic of the circus he had grown accustomed to living in.

Five minutes later, Brant and Nico were feeding cheese puffs into Gus's mouth to keep xer from growling while Paula was grabbing tools from the garage. Both Eddie and Laszlo had started prying the doorframe apart and doing some very gentle demolition to the wood while trying not to aggravate the dragon. Gus appeared to be both mollified by the bribes but also self-conscious of being stuck, so was not at xer's best around the strangers. Eddie and Laszlo both were slowed somewhat by wearing thick gloves Brant kept on hand in case Gus changed xer's mind and decided to snap at one of them. The tight spot didn't help matters of maneuverability.

Eventually, Gus was freed, and everyone breathed a sigh of relief as xer dropped to xer's claws on the floor. Eddie and Laszlo were sweaty and dusty from the effort but seemed to take it in stride. Nico pointed one to the upstairs bathroom to freshen up, while the other went into the second bathroom off Brant's room. The moment Gus was free, xer went to the living room to curl up, sulking over the undignified experience. Brant didn't need to even ask; Nico went right over to comfort Gus, and Brant headed back outside to attempt, again, to introduce their crazy little family to a yard full of strangers.

As Brant walked through the carport, he thought to himself, *I wonder if we could bribe the tribunal with cheesy snacks. Or cookies.*

Attitude: Scale of 1–5, 5 being very happy. Up and Down with lightning speed. 1/5/2/4.5.

Behavior: Tantrums now manifest by Gus turning certain body parts to stone. Pull of persuasive magic now extends to Midwest and East Coast.

Changes in weight, body shape, color, extremities: Weight is approx 140 lbs. Color has been changing to evergreen. Scales are tougher.

Communication: With me, uses visions at night (mostly) to leave "impressions" employing both scent, sound, and touch. Watches a voracious amount of global channels in all kinds of languages. Has sent through a few key phrases. But with Brant, communicates through grunts, groans, awoo's and chuffs. With Paula, likes to bump her legs and hips for attention. Has enjoyed all the new company. A lot.

Changes in motor function, diet, and sleep:
Dexterity is off the charts. Can walk almost
silently for size, which is astonishing. Has flexed
wings a few times in attempt to fly. Diet is now
full turkeys, whole chickens. We have started to
supplement with a kind of dragon-friendly
meatloaf after a bunch of trial and error. Gus
doesn't like it, but will eat it if there are
cheese puffs on top. We have discovered xer has
a taste for chocolate cake. Sleep is very
erratic. Sometimes xer sleeps through the day,
but sometimes wakes and cries pitifully.

CHAPTER 14

Late May to Mid-June

The chaotic tone of the next few weeks continued as the days flew by, the tribunal date looming larger on the calendar every day. Newcomers arrived in a steady stream and Brant and Nico tried to help each of them adjust as best they could. Not everyone stayed in Multnomah, of course, but even the ones who had decided to return to their lives were still spending time with their household and exploring the city like a mini vacation. Nico thought momentarily that he was going to have to sedate Brant when a yarn wholesaler by the name of Cecilia Fullilove showed up. Cecilia was a Black Creole woman from Louisiana, good-natured and bright, and she laughed with her whole body. She had a sunny disposition and she and Brant became instant friends. Brant managed to wrangle a promise from Cecilia that he could have first pick of the latest organic, blue-dyed batch of baby alpaca wool. When she surprised him a few days later, he immediately began knitting with the yarn during stolen moments of peace, his eyes furrowed in concentration over his new project.

The new recruits continued to arrive with eclectic backgrounds and lifestyles. There was Koda the veterinarian, an Indian transwoman who kept bringing up lizard facts. After checking with Gus, Koda was allowed to examine xer and take notes, which was surprising, as Gus typically didn't enjoy scrutiny by anyone but xer's dads. Arriving at the same time as Koda were Cyr and Neil. Cyr was a tall Persian goth woman who drove subway trains in New York. She had an imposing air, but when she met Gus, her smile lit up the room. Nico particularly enjoyed meeting Neil, a writer with bushy black hair and a serious face. Neil and Nico bonded over their mutual love of journaling. They sat huddled in the corner of the living room on more than a few occasions, scribbling, reciting, and occasionally sharing each other's work.

Brant had set up a messaging system in order to stay in touch with everyone who was still in town and kept a faithful catalog of who was going back to their respective cities. He guarded this list carefully, carrying it with him everywhere. He knew that the information, if leaked, could cause more havoc than they were prepared to handle.

Nico awoke the day of his date with Bisan to the feeling of butterflies in his stomach. He moved about in a daze and pulled at his nice, collared shirt, one of the only ones in his closet that was free from dirt and mud stains. Just as Nico was leaving, Brant tugged wordlessly on his sleeve, looking his friend over appraisingly. Brant didn't say anything as he straightened Nico's shirt, but Nico still registered the smug look on Brant's face before he left. He heard a soft, "Just be yourself," as the door clicked shut.

As he pulled up to the coffee shop where they were to meet, Nico gently lifted the bouquet of fireweed he had put together. He was more accustomed to growing plants and helping them thrive, but he didn't want to give Bisan something to take care of if, God forbid, she had a black thumb. As he walked in the door, a small bell tinkled his arrival overhead. Nico didn't know how he knew, but he knew where she would be and found her instantly. She smiled warmly as their eyes met, and suddenly shy, Nico averted his gaze as he made his way over, offering the cut flowers to her. She was still smiling as she took the flowers and asked, "Now that the scary bit is over, we can go order."

"The scary bit?" Nico asked, puzzled.

"Yeah. Making sure you actually showed up." She winked at him and looped her arm in his, pulling him towards the counter. Nico was speechless at the idea that someone would stand up such a beautiful person.

As they settled with their drinks and pastries, the conversation moved like a trickling stream at first, then picked up pace as the questions came. Bisan was curious about Nico's passion for all things green, asking about his views on the environment and ecosystems. He warmed to the subject slowly but caught himself impassioned about the value of bees and other pollinators in the life cycle, his arms moving in the air with excitement. Bisan only shook her head, pleased and saying nothing. He turned the conversation to her, as he was just as curious about how she found her passion for teaching. She described her love for education at a young age, lining up her younger siblings to teach them how to brush their hair and teeth, little faces solemn as they took direction from their big sister seriously.

They exchanged stories from their lives with more ease than Nico had thought possible. Even his friendship with Brant had never felt this effortless. There was a charge of attraction that had lingered in the air between them, and Nico's heart grew bolder with every passing minute. The time flew by over the whole afternoon.

A few hours later, Nico decided to break the news of Gus to her gently. "I do have something important to talk to you about, just so you know what you are getting into."

Bisan had been staring out the window during a lull in the conversation and turned back to him. She reached across the table and took his hand, giving it a reassuring squeeze. Nico's heart beat wildly in his chest, but he waited. *Patience*, he thought.

Bisan said softly, "Are you going to tell me about the dragon?"

"You knew?" Nico asked, baffled. "I take it you listen to the radio, then," he said, a bitter edge to his voice.

Her fingers shifted and danced across the back of his hand, making him laugh at the tickle. She smiled at him and continued, "No, but there's enough buzz around town about it, and then there's how cryptic you've been. I am a smart cookie, I put two and two together."

"It's a relief that you know about Gustopher. Even if some of it is probably wild conspiracy theories. It does mean that things are up in the air for me right now. Can I tell you a little bit about Gus?"

She nodded and listened with rapt attention to some of the stories that had happened in the last few months. Nico didn't tell her everything, but shared what he felt was some of Gus's best attributes. Xer's kindness and playfulness. Xer's wisdom, and intuition. As she listened, she toyed with her necklace. It was made of chunky lapis lazuli stones but suddenly while Nico was mid-sentence, the thread snapped and the beads began rolling everywhere, across the table, booth seats, and the cafe floor. Nico leapt into action and began chasing the semiprecious stones. As he dashed back and forth, Bisan's gasp of surprise and delight rang out across the space. She clapped with relief as Nico recovered every one of the necklace pieces, and they leaned in, puzzling back together every link of the necklace on the thread while talking softly. It was a wonderful afternoon.

Over the next few days, it was evident that Gus had grown almost completely out of xer's awkward size and goofy mannerisms. Xer had also grown sleeker and stealthier, and xer's appetite was off the charts. The sheer volume of food and waste took many hands to manage. Thankfully, Brant and Nico were never handling things just on their own these days. The house had a steady stream of now-familiar faces that were in constant motion. The kitchen was always clean, the floors were always swept. Gus was always fed, thankfully, and given plenty of attention. Even the post-Gus food waste was put to good use, because, as it turns out, dragon fertilizer is very potent for composting.

The size issue was becoming their biggest problem, next to the looming town hall. The expanded door frame leading to the basement was a stark reminder of that. Despite the infrequency of it, there were also still moments where Gus acted out. Dr. Laborn had come by a second time to try and convince them that turning over Gus could lead to "life-saving cures for who knows how many illnesses." While both Nico and Brant weren't sure of their future with Gus, that was not an option they would entertain. Afterward, Gus made xer's feelings about the visit known by throwing a tantrum and setting part of the kitchen cabinet and floor on fire. It was a small fire, and no one was hurt, but Brant was so upset over the damage to his grandmother's house that he wouldn't speak to or acknowledge Gus for several days until the repairs were done.

There was also a second instance where Gus would not cooperate after a very pleasant evening with a small group of newcomers. Everyone was sprawled about in the living room, snack trays and bags everywhere. Gus was in the center of the floor surrounded on all sides, xer's head resting on Charles the mechanic, xer's tail curled around Wali the nurse's arm, and xer's front claws were tucked underneath Oded's legs.

Nico and Brant had put a movie on and several hours passed in a cozy and relaxed atmosphere with a group of about eight people. Once a few of them had begun yawning and shifting after the movie to pack up and call it a night, Brant turned the movie off. Gus was not happy that the evening had come to an end and responded by turning xer's front and back feet to stone. Oded had yelped at the feel of cold marble suddenly against the backs of his legs and jumped up.

Ke Fuy must've also been resting against Gus, because he too gave an astonished shout and stood quickly. Brant and Nico were confused at first, as they couldn't identify the alarm. Oded and Ke Fuy both moved out of the living room.

"What is THAT?!" Oded shouted, with a bark of disbelief, pointing at Gus's feet.

Brant scanned Oded first to see if he was injured, then looked over at Gus. He saw his kid's feet in solid concrete blocks, claws flexed, fading into Gus's deep green legs and body. Only the last few inches of xer had turned to rock. Brant rolled his eyes at Gus in exasperation.

"Seriously, dude! We were about to end on such a high note! And here you are, throwing a tantrum because you want a sleepover!" Brant glanced furtively at Oded and saw the musician had raised an eyebrow meaningfully.

Nico covered a disbelieving laugh with a cough. He couldn't believe Gus's antics, but he also couldn't believe

Brant had said his internal thoughts out loud. He turned to Gus, with perfect deadpan sarcasm, "Yeah, Gus. How could you. Oh, no. What a terrible turn of events."

Brant gave Nico a look that clearly said, *You are not helping.*

Nico returned the unspoken look with raised eyebrows and a gleeful look, *Actually, I am.*

Everyone besides Nico and Brant shifted to the dining room and kitchen while the dads conferred. Gus just lay there, eyes closed in satisfaction, wearing a smug, superior expression. The two men whispered strategies as to how to get Gus to revert xer's feet back to flesh. Bribing with Gus's favorite treats didn't work. Flattery didn't work, though Oded gave it a valiant effort by calling Gus "a gift to all humankind, wise and radiant." Brant even tried picking Gus up bodily, a bad idea from the start. This ended an otherwise wonderful evening with a scowling dragon who made xer's displeasure known at bedtime by rumbling sonic waves across the basement ominously. As Oded was leaving, he tried to reassure Brant that it had still been a glorious night. Brant just wrinkled his nose in frustration.

The mayor's office had also tried calling a few times and left messages on their voicemails, friendly at first, but with increasing urgency to call him back. Nico wondered what connection the mayor had to the magic tribunal and made a note to ask Ms. Marguerita before June 21st. He had requested that Ms. Marguerita come back for a brief visit before then, as he had more questions for her.

Because of all the distractions around Gus, the vibe of the whole house became more reserved despite the occasional sweet moments.

Nico observed and recorded these changes as usual but had started to see a pattern emerge. The more people that Gus drew to xer, the more xer's powers seem to amplify. Xer was still sending out the mysterious sonic pulse sometimes, but it was subtler, deeper, and shorter. Xer moved with more grace, had stronger wings, and there was no point locking drawers or doors anymore. There wasn't a human-made lock that Gus couldn't pick with xer's claws. The dexterity had seemed to come overnight. While there hadn't been a need to go invisible again — and Gus's dads were in no hurry to test that, given how frightening it was last time — Nico suspected that Gus could use that power with little to no consequence, if the potency of the other abilities was any indication. He wondered for the thousandth time exactly what Gus's affinity was. The broad range of people that Gus had attracted made it a puzzle that Nico wanted to solve.

On the evening before the summer solstice, Brant and Nico were in the kitchen with Oded, Koda, Hermengildo, Sylvester, and Terri the magician. Brant and Nico had explained to all the newcomers that they couldn't come to the town hall as there should be as few humans as possible. Many of them understood that it was dangerous and could damage the outcome of the judgment but were understandably worried and eager to be of help. The group gathered in the kitchen was staying close by for as long as possible to be supportive, which Brant and Nico were grateful for.

With the house full these days, it made Nico remember when Remi, Jasper, and all the hockey guys were around. Though they still hadn't heard from any of them in the last several months, Nico missed them and wondered if, at the very least, Remi was getting their messages. Remi had made it clear that he was anathema to vampires for shunning the drinking of human blood. Nico wondered if Remi knew the vampire who was on the tribunal personally. He knew that Gus was missing Remi, too. Gus hadn't communicated anything specific; it was just a feeling in his gut.

Later, Gus gave xer's customary head bump to both dads and went carefully down the basement stairs. This was unusual behavior for Gus, as xer was typically awake well into the nocturnal hours. Brant and Nico took this as a sign of stress but there wasn't much to do other than follow suit, as the next evening was going to be a defining one.

That evening, Nico dreamed deeply.

Chapter 15

Gus lay in a deep, cragged cavern high up a rocky mountain, too exhausted to even find food or start a fire to keep warm. Xer took a few labored breaths, trying to calm the rage that burned in xer's heart. For thousands of years, they had peace. The last hundred years, however, humans had turned away completely from their friends in nature. The wolves had gone deeper into the forests and valleys. The bears retreated as well, some even headed north to areas that humans could barely survive in, areas of frozen tundra with ice as deep as the imagination could go. And the dragons...well. The dragons were still trying, trying desperately to connect to humanity. They had all had such a fruitful relationship for so long, and now, what? They were hunted for sport. Lies had spread about a dragon's greed for gold. Xer snorted in laughter at the very idea. As if dragons cared about material things. Relationships with others was deeply ingrained in a dragon's soul. It made all of the turmoil and disaster worth it: to connect, to help each other. To build prosperity and create innovation.

Hadn't the dragons done enough to help build human civilization? The architecture dragon helped to inspire their...what were they called, churches? Their music dragon brought on a revolution of sound that was echoing throughout the continents. It had birthed something humans called 'the Renaissance.' The art and sculpture dragons had been so busy, Gus hadn't seen them at all in over 30 human years. But Gus's talent...it was still so controversial. It had taken xer a long, long time to understand what exactly was at the heart of xer's talent. This was less evident in other species but in humans, the evidence was plain. Gus magnetically drew to xer gender abundance, more, much more than that of the narrow view of male and female.

Gus glanced back at the humans with xer and regretted getting lost in thought and leaving them shivering in the cold and dark cave. Xer used mindspeak, comforting them with reassurances that they would not be caught here. As Gus did so, xer lit some brittle, dry branches that had blown in from a storm. Soon, a fire was blazing, and the humans were able to relax and unpack their hastily assembled satchels.

Gus watched with a soul weariness xer had never felt before. Among these humans was a typical sampling of what xer's affinity drew out: a diversity of their species' genders. There were androgynes and intersex. Non-binary and transgender. There were calabai and bissu with xer tonight, and a eunuch as well. And the humans were all shapes, sizes, and ages, too. Some had barely escaped death during persecution, bearing the terrible cost on their bodies. Some were missing limbs; some could not see or hear.

The eldest among them was a very, very old gender fluid person who had lost their hearing many years before after getting caught in a rockslide in their hometown. They were only a young adult at the time it happened, but they were shunned by their village as no longer useful to the tribe as a whole, even though this human had a gift for wielding metal that rivaled other blacksmiths within 100 leagues. Gus had seen other villages who used a complicated series of hand gestures to communicate when one of their own could not hear, but this village would not take Gus's suggestion, and instead, chose to banish the youth.

That youth was now an elder who could communicate quite deeply with Gus, and for that, Gus was grateful.

Each member of this group had a similar story and had sought out Gus and dragonkind to protect them, even as the humans ridiculed and banished them. Gus had protected them as best xer could for many years, but the dragon-hunting had increased more and more, making it impossible to hide. Dragons and the humans who associated with them were called evil, branded with outlandish lies and called witches and spellcasters. Some even claimed that they were possessed by demons.

The very idea that dragons and the orphans who **humans themselves** had cast out had anything more than a desire to live peaceably and be among community was so ludicrous that it made Gus enraged.

Xer looked around at the gathered group. They couldn't all travel together like this anymore. It wasn't safe for the humans. Gus was too much of a target and there were more and more dragon hunters every passing moon.

Gus mindspoke to the elder.

'I have to leave you. It is not safe any longer. I know where you can go.'

They replied, 'What hope do we have, if you leave?'

'Go to the islands in the center of the Peaceful Ocean. The journey will be very hard, but the people there will welcome all of you. They call it Mokupuni Hawai'i.'

'What will you do?'

'I will hibernate and hope for a better day ahead. For all of us,' Gus finished sadly. Gus was looking down, unable to meet their eyes. Xer felt like such a failure but couldn't see another way for xer's beloveds to survive. Gus felt a human hand on xer's shoulder, strong and reassuring.

'You will always be our protector. There will always be a need for you. Come back when you can, when you think humans will end their hate for others.'

'Could be a long time,' Gus thought dryly, shaking xer's head.

'What is time, to a dragon?'' they smiled, and the radiant love in it nearly broke Gus's heart in two. Gus had said this to them on so many occasions as a way to say, we will weather this, too.

The elder communicated to the others that Gus was leaving, and there was a rush of bodies as everyone in the cave embraced Gus tightly. Gus could feel their fear and desperation, but underneath it all, the *impossibly vast vibration of love and strength. They would make it to the islands, they would live out their lives in peace.*

But for Gus, it would be a different road. One that had been talked about among dragonkind since they came into being. Xer's kind had experimented with hibernation in secret, never to be shared with humans. It was a last resort, only to be used in the case of direst emergency as a way to survive the planet's natural calamities. Gus, being the oldest among dragons, had been the first to experiment with it and had survived the process. It was easy to begin and slow to undo, but it could be done. The transformation magics were strange to manipulate, and it took a sense of despair that dragons typically didn't have. Until now. Each dragon had to know in xer's heart that there was no other choice.

Nico awoke with a start and sat bolt upright in bed. He looked at the clock and blinked blearily until his eyes adjusted. The clock read a little after 2 a.m. He touched his face and was surprised to find tears there. He put on his slippers and headed downstairs to make a cup of tea. As he tiptoed quietly down, he spotted Brant in the kitchen, standing at the island, tears rolling down his face. He heard Nico approach and without a word, walked over and hugged him tightly.

"Did you have it, too?" Nico asked softly, just to confirm it wasn't something else. He felt Brant nod into his shoulder. This was Brant's first experience with one of Gus's visions, and he was visibly shaken.

"The others weren't like this one," Nico said, keeping his voice low. He was still feeling the vast grief of Gus having to leave his favorite humans, feeling as if xer failed them. He drew a shaky breath and pulled gently from Brant's grip. He squeezed his shoulder and said, "Tea. We need tea," and set about brewing two cups of calming chamomile with a teaspoon of lavender honey.

10 minutes later, both men were seated on the couch facing each other under some blankets tossed at their feet and sleepily talking about what the vision meant. Slowly, with the faint light from the kitchen barely falling on their faces, both their heads dropped, and they fell back asleep.

Gus awoke after a fitful night of sleep with the humans for a few hours. It was still very, very early in the morning, and xer could hear the owls hooting on their hunts as they passed the high outcrop of the cave. Xer glanced for a long moment among xer's family, xer's kin. Then despite the fire of love emblazoned on xer's heart, Gus stealthily crept to the edge of the cave to leave them all, only stopping briefly to warm the fire just a little with xer's breath. A little gift to keep them all sleeping longer. Not a sound could be heard as Gus moved. Even the elder slept deeply, huddled and protected by the others.

Gus turned back to the opening of the cave, straining xer's senses, on alert for any sign of danger, but there were only the nighttime creatures, scuttling about their business.

Gus took flight, spreading xer's enormous wings, and never looked back.

Gus flew for several hours, using xer's ability to manipulate light around xer, to shield the vision of xer's frame against the night sky. Gus knew where to go; it was ironic, really. All of this time hiding from the humans and going to remote places that was hard for them to breathe in, to climb to, to be comfortable in. Xer had decided in a fit of rebellion that if dragonkind was going to be exiled for association with outcast humans then xer would hide in plain sight. If Gus knew humans at all then they wouldn't even see them. Xer could hibernate and watch with xer's mind's-eye, waiting for the right time to reconnect, to build community and diversity. To celebrate interspecies friendships and alliances.

Gus landed silently on the roof of a soaring cathedral. Xer had sent out a few messages among the dragons that xer knew were hiding along the flight path, rolling a sonic wave out that sounded like thunder to the human ear. A few other dragons heard the call and landed just as silently near xer on the rooftop. They had all agreed long ago that if one of them ever chose to hibernate, xer would not do it alone. The other dragons all nodded at Gus; they were ready. Gus looked long at each of them, drinking in their faces and bodies. It was the last look Gus would have of them for a long, long time. Xer wanted it to carry xer throughout the centuries. No dragon knew how long a hibernation might take.

Gus began the transformation magics, shifting and squeezing, delicately rearranging cells, sending some of xer's essence into the ether, some into the plane-beyond, anchoring only a fraction of xer's power and soul. **Just enough***, xer thought. Just enough to stay alive. Just enough to let the heart beat and conscious thought listen to the civilization below. From up here, Gus and the others could watch the city rise, watch its population swell, its food stores grow, and rivers fill with boats. They could see the progress and the setbacks. They could see art and love, sex and science, traditions and customs, paranoia and war.*

As the stone texture started at Gus's feet, xer stepped out onto the ledge, curling xer's claws around the edge menacingly. The stone had traveled up Gus's spine, giving xer a posture of aggressive threat. Gus could feel the cold stone closing around xer's soft cheeks. Xer's mouth opened wide in a snarl of defiance. One of Gus's last thoughts was...

Nico and Brant both woke up at the same time. A sliver of dawn could be seen through the curtains. No one on their street was stirring yet, but they were. Gus was standing in the living room on all fours, staring at Brant and Nico.

And then the words from the end of the vision came, so fierce and so defiant, Nico and Brant clapped their hands over their ears, though the voice came from within, deep and gravely. Foreign, guttural, and yet familiar. It was firm and absolute. Gustopher the dragon, who'd been alive for thousands of years, said,

"WE. WILL NOT. BE SILENCED."

CHAPTER 16

June 21ˢᵗ, Summer Solstice

Nico and Brant spent the entire day in a daze. Koffe called to confirm what time his van should be there to take Gus to the town hall, but Brant couldn't process what he was saying. Thankfully, Brant had thought a few weeks ago to arrange everything in advance. He suspected that they might be caught off-guard by something at the last minute. They were both so stunned by the vision they had shared the night before that they barely had the presence of mind to get showered and dressed.

The influx of newcomers had also brought the benefit of people available to work the cookie truck at all hours. This made it easy for Brant to focus on the production rather than the selling aspect of the cookie truck. Now faced with the idea that Gus might leave them that evening after the judgment of the tribunal, all of them were dealing with it in their own way. Gus spent xer's time evenly split between them, either shadowing Brant in the kitchen or curled up with Nico and his papers, journals, and reference books. He was trying frantically to find something in Ms. Marguerita's academic papers that would assist in filling in more lore, even as it was still developing. Ms. Marguerita was nothing if not shrewd, making sure that Nico would have everything he needed to continue documenting history in the making.

The day passed by in a blur. Suddenly, it was almost 9:30 p.m. and time to pack up and make the drive.

Koffe and Brant helped guide Gustopher into Koffe's van, which had been cleared out and swept clean. A nice rug had been put down, a thoughtful touch. Nico's throat grew tight as he considered that they might be driving back without Gus in the van. He hated the feeling that anyone had a right to decide what was best for Gus unless it was...well, Gustopher. Xer had grown so much in the last four months. The magic, the people, the love and the care had all helped Gus come fully back into xer's powers, and xer certainly didn't need their protection anymore. Nico wondered what Gus was thinking now as Koffe drove off with Gus in the back, completely obscured by the van's darkened windows. Brant, Nico and Ms. Marguerita piled into Nico's minivan, caravaning behind them.

Nico had a few more questions for Ms. Marguerita and knew this might be his last chance to speak with her directly. He wasted no time, turning in his seat and addressing her.

"So, do you work exclusively with the tribunal here?"

Ms. Marguerita gave Nico a piercing look.

"I am a visiting scholar, so to speak. I travel to many places to work with magickind on their various disputes."

"Does that mean the question of dragons has come up before, in other places?" Nico pressed as much as he dared.

Ms. Marguerita glanced at Brant, who risked a look away from the road to see her response. She reached into her purse and pulled out a business card. She handed it to Nico, closing her bag with a sharp snap. She said, "You know that I can only answer certain questions at this point. My knowledge is bound, at the moment, based on the agreement I have with the tribunal. However, *when this is all over,* contact me and I can speak more freely as to my larger purpose." She gave Nico a penetrating stare. He turned back in his seat, studying the card and tucking it carefully in his pocket.

Brant decided to change the subject. "What about the tribunal itself? Can you tell us more about them?" he asked as respectfully as possible.

Ms. Marguerita folded her hands in her lap and her lips tightened. She addressed Brant in her classic, no-nonsense manner. "Young man, I am not your personal encyclopedia. If you want to know about your region's magickind and their rules, you should have spent some time at the library." She bristled and rotated her shoulders restlessly. "Although," she mused, "I suppose keeping Gus out of the public eye has made such trips more challenging," she paused, considering. Brant looked over at Nico and shrugged as if to say, *I tried.* Nico nodded back.

"I will tell you a few things," she announced. "The different magical species that make up your region are a blend of pixies, centaurs, vampires, werewolves, witches, dwarves, a very small population of goblins, and obviously at least one dragon. They co-exist through treaties which are often broken and result in minor squabbles. Those smaller disputes are typically resolved with a local magistrate — your tribunal — through trade and offerings. When a larger event happens that impacts more than one region, a scholar like myself is brought in," she scowled briefly. "The tribunal also works with the local human government, but this is largely to keep the worlds as separate as possible. For safety." She gazed out the window, lost in thought.

Brant, in an attempt to keep her talking, prompted, "So why do they use terms like an animal's life cycle to denote time?"

Ms. Marguerita gave a snort. "The magical species of our world have longer life spans than humans and spend 90% of their time in nature, with a few exceptions. The concept of hours, minutes...even months is very perplexing to them. They see how you built your world around it, especially in relation to how many engines surround human civilization, but they simply don't *like* it. They can reckon time the way we do, but they look down on it."

Brant and Nico both nodded along. Nico was beginning to see how complicated it was to do her job. Understanding the nuances of magickind meant knowing what each species valued, how they communicated, and what resentments lay in their prejudices. He didn't envy Ms. Marguerita her job. He admired her dedication to the communication between so many species and their cultures.

Soon they were pulling up to a remote field in the middle of nowhere. Brant, Nico, and Koffe all assembled and released Gus from the back of the van while Ms. Marguerita stood nearby, gazing into the forest. The agreement was that Koffe would wait with the vehicles at the edge of the field while the rest of them went to the town hall. Koffe was strictly forbidden from speaking of where they were, or even to watch the direction the rest of them were walking in. He agreed readily and gave Gustopher an awkward pat on the shoulder before turning back to climb into the van.

The four of them stepped further into the field, letting Ms. Marguerita take the lead. As they approached the tree line of the forest on the other side of the field, Nico could see a shimmering ripple where the light was bending. The forest looked as ordinary as ever and yet there was a quality to it that seemed a little off. He was also getting a strong urge to leave, though the evening was lovely, and he was with his favorite people. He chalked it up to his nerves. There was no reason to want to leave, and yet, Nico felt the desire even more strongly the closer they approached the trees. Brant looked over at Nico and was shaking his head as if to say, *No, we shouldn't go in there.* Nico nodded back and just shrugged, glancing at Ms. Marguerita for reassurance. But the Italian woman walked purposefully straight into the forest, muttering a few words as they approached. She waved her hands in a complicated series of circles and jabs, and as soon as they reached the darkened canopy, the view shifted.

Nico expected the lights from the truck and van to dim as they walked under the cover of the evergreen pines and for the ground to be damp from the leaves, moss, and deadfall strewn about. It was not unusual for the forested areas of Multnomah to still be damp and chilly even leading right into summer. But here the ground was as warm and firm as the packed dirt of a country road on a sunny summer day. They must've crossed a magical threshold of some kind; as the illusion of the forest faded away, the light was a blend of the dark blues and purples of a clear, starry sky combined with the glow of the full moon, high at its zenith. And there, bursting with life, was a thriving night market, buzzing with trade. The market itself threw off colors of bright yellows from the lamps and shimmering draped lights that zig-zagged across the path. The canopies were alternating between deep jewel tones of emerald green, saffron, blood red, and rich oak-bark brown.

Nico could see stalls overloaded with products, vendors shaking their goods, and shouting for barter at passersby. Brant gaped at the creatures that went past; some were werewolves that must've been 7 feet tall, thudding along the ground on their hind feet and shaking the earth with their paws. One sneered at the two men, but when it saw Ms. Marguerita, gave a solemn nod of respect. Nico could see flying pixies, darting about playfully in the air, throwing tiny red berries at each other, the ammunition landing on patrons' heads, who brushed away the juicy lumps with irritation.

Brant counted at least four species of magickind he hadn't even heard of, and as he reached out to touch their guide on the shoulder to ask her about it, she shot both of them a warning glance, holding up her index finger as a command. *Be quiet,* was the plain gesture.

Nico contented himself with taking in the booths, the music, the strange languages, and the new smells. His fingers itched for his journal to record the sights. He was almost too distracted to stop dreading the tribunal. He glanced down at Gus and noticed that the dragon was also soaking up the atmosphere. Gustopher's eyes were lit up with intrigue and excitement. A lump formed in the pit of his stomach as he realized that though it might mean not seeing Gus again, being among magickind would at least give Gus the kind of life xer deserved. Several creatures stared at all of them as they walked — especially Gus — but at the sight of Ms. Marguerita, more of them dipped their heads with a nod of reverential respect.

Nico and Brant both followed Ms. Marguerita faithfully through the market, winding their way deeper and deeper into the woods. As they got further away from the entry point, the paths became quieter, the vendors a bit more menacing. There were potion bottles and weapons here, illusion clothing and books so dangerous, they were covered in glass domes. Nico could make out traces of glittering light snakes that circled these forbidden objects. They were drifting lazily in the air around the glass like miniature undulating fireworks, opening their jaws and roaring periodically to warn innocent hands not to stray. They were about the size of a garden snake but looked infinitely more deadly. Nico had no desire to test whatever magic held those books at bay, nor to mess with the light-serpents. Gus, however, leaped forward to bite at them the way a puppy would try to bite snowflakes.

They had finally made their way past the market proper where there was a clearing of ancient redwood trees in a semi-circle. Arranged in a crescent moon, facing the market were six chairs, their backs to the enormous trees. Across from the tribunal member chairs was a guest table with three seats and a raised platform for Gus to lie on comfortably. Here the sky was completely open past the soaring tree line, the stars overhead barely visible under the radiant moon bathing the clearing in pale blue light. There were a few faint torches around the edges, but the moonlight made it bright as day.

This area was clearly where they were headed, as there were already tribunal members present, seated in the chairs in silence. Ms. Marguerita guided Brant and Nico to the guest table, and Nico whispered softly to Gus to lie down, and xer did so without resistance. As Nico leaned down to reassure Gus, he looked into Gus's eyes and saw a note of amusement there. It seemed impossible to Nico that even in their most serious moment, when they all might be separated, Gus could find something to smile about. Xer ducked xer's face under Nico's chin and gave the slightest, most gentle bump. Nico's jaw clacked slightly, and he let out a soft laugh in return.

Straightening up, Nico settled into the nearest chair and risked a glance at the gathered magical folks. He could see the three that Brant had described from months ago: a small and elderly pixie with a mohawk full of bright colors; a werewolf with a bushy purple beard, his arms crossed on his giant hairy chest; and a lounging but deadly vampire woman who had a leg draped over the arm of her chair, oblivious to everyone else. She was filing her nails nonchalantly. There was a chair that seemed both occupied and not at the same time; a vapor was drifting in and out of the spot where someone would — theoretically — sit. Brant could make out a face in the mist that seemed vaguely female, but the clarity of her features was fading in and out.

Nico felt the pit of dread he'd been fighting for weeks. None of anything he'd experienced so far could prepare him for the sheer power of magic in this space, the sense of authority here. He felt small and ignorant. He felt terrified and angry, and terribly helpless. He looked at Brant and saw the same feelings reflected there. Brant was struggling to keep his rebellious nature under wraps. Their best chance was to let Ms. Marguerita do her job. She tapped on the table, giving them both a steely gaze and gestured toward the occupied-yet-not chair.

Ms. Marguerita leaned over to whisper, "That is Crittenden. She is a witch who died many hundreds of years ago. She is from the spirit realm, but on matters as important as this, she is in attendance. So be respectful and don't stare. It takes unspeakable power to cross the veil."

Brant and Nico both nodded their understanding. Ms. Marguerita continued softly, "We are waiting for two more members. Remember, you will not speak. I will present the reasons to the tribunal, both in favor of you and against you. I am charged with being thorough, so don't interrupt me. Trust I have all the information *meant to be shared,*" she emphasized, looking at Brant sharply. Brant nodded his head again in agreement, understanding her strategy. Brant reached out to squeeze Nico's arm in support. Nico patted him on the back in return.

Ms. Marguerita continued, "As I said before, the judgment will go one of three ways: Gus may be allowed to stay; Xer may be moved to a magical family, not one of xer's kin, but at least those who can feed and house xer comfortably until xer is fully grown and able to express powers. The final, and less likely option, is that Gus will be released into the wilds."

"How would they take Gus from us?" Brant asked bluntly. Ms. Marguerita looked at Brant with something resembling sympathy, murmuring her response. "The enforcers of the tribunal are the rangers. They have a method of neutralizing the magical abilities of any magical species who are being transported or who are resisting being relocated. It doesn't harm them, but the word neutralization conjures irritation for some and downright panic for others," she said, frowning slightly. "I am unsure of how Gus will react, or if it will even work on xer, but trust that they are nearby —even though you cannot see them — and ready as soon as the tribunal makes its decision," she concluded.

Brant hated this. To sit in a chair and do nothing to protect his ward, his beloved Gustopher? He had found this kid in a time of great vulnerability. He wasn't sure what was best, but why were these folks making decisions about his life and family without him being able to speak about it? He raged internally, struggling to keep his temper under control. It was more likely that his desire to speak out would just put his foot in his mouth. He glanced at Nico who wore a look of infinite sadness.

Nico had no hope for them to keep Gus and had already accepted it, but Brant was not quite there yet. He kept thinking that there must be some hare-brained, reckless thing he could do to get all three of them out and away. His desire to run had never been strong before; he was more of a stand-and-fight kind of guy. But now? It was all he could do to keep from bolting out of his chair, grabbing Gus and Nico, and making a beeline for Koffe, the van, and the open road.

Ms. Marguerita, as usual, seemed to be able to read Brant's mind and fixed him with a look that made it clear he was to do no such thing. Brant closed his eyes and counted to 10, slowing his breathing as much as he could to quell his raging heart. Once he had calmed down a little, he asked her, "So who else are we waiting for? I thought we had to be here strictly on time."

Ms. Marguerita was looking among the tribunal, a couple of whom were leaning in and whispering amongst themselves. The pixie was looking distracted at the market behind them, and the werewolf and the lady-of-vapor were both stirring restlessly in their seats. Only the vampire continued to ignore them all, looking utterly bored and filing her long, long nails into razor-sharp points. She occasionally gave Gus an appraising look and her eyes held a gleam of greed. Gus, in return, stared back menacingly. He let out the lowest of growls, rumbling a sound wave so deep the werewolf's ears flattened back, and he looked at Gus, startled.

Suddenly, at the back of the clearing, there was a commotion from the crowd. The night market vendors and shoppers surged forward through the narrow path, spilling into the clearing but not quite stepping in fully. There was an invisible barrier the crowd understood; this was an area of judgment they did *not* want to be at the mercy of. Still, the disruption was big enough that the chaos increased and sounds of arguing could be heard.

Gus stood and craned around, curious. Brant and Nico also rose in their chairs, peering into the gloom to see what had caused the disturbance.

Chapter 17

The crowd was making it hard to see who was at the center, but slowly and awkwardly three men pushed through and stood at the edge of the clearing. The crowd melted back, not wanting to face the potential anger of the tribunal. Two of the men were enormous bodyguards wearing black suits and earpieces, which they tapped periodically in frustration. *Their audio equipment must be affected by the illusion spell*, Brant thought. The two men were flanking a tall, slender white man who wore an expensive suit and tie. He was in his mid-30s approximately, with conservatively styled black hair and blue eyes. He was waving his hands around as if he were greeting an enthusiastic crowd. Brant realized with a start that this was the mayor, the man who'd been trying to reach them for weeks. He recognized him from the newspaper articles. *No wonder he thinks he's the most important person in the room*, Brant thought, intrigued. *This ought to be interesting.*

Nico glanced at Ms. Marguerita and saw that she was utterly astonished and breathtakingly angry. Her eyes flashed and her hands were clenched. Her mouth opened and closed a few times, but she was gathering herself to speak. The man smiled toothily as he walked over to her without a care in the world and patted her condescendingly on the shoulder.

Most of the tribunal stared at the man with open irritation but the vampire woman finally shifted from her careless,

"

relaxed position to leaning with her elbows on her knees, templing her fingers together and baring all of her teeth.

He addressed everyone present, even the crowd behind him with a sweep of his hand.

"Good tidings! I am Mayor Flint and I have to come to declare that this proceeding cannot commence, as it violates the treaty between our kind that was enacted over..." he paused as one of his bodyguards murmured something low in his ear, "one least weasel lifespan ago."[2]

This announcement was followed by a deafening silence. The tribunal was caught off-guard by the mayor's disrespect and arrogance at interrupting and making declarations unsanctioned by *them*. Ms. Marguerita was not having any of it, and she spoke to the mayor directly.

"Sir, I can appreciate that you feel you have some sort of say of what goes on in the Multnomah region, but as you can see, this falls under our purview and so —"

Mayor Flint raised his hand to interrupt her. He walked over to Gus and smiled appreciatively. He looked like a cat who was about to eat a bird. Gus's expression was hard to discern. Xer looked wary and a bit angry, but xer did not respond to the mayor. Mayor Flint finally made eye contact with Brant and Nico, and Brant swore he could detect a note of glee in his voice as he spoke. *He's making a spectacle on purpose,* he thought. *He's putting them on the spot,* he reflected. *Good.*

"As I was saying, these proceedings are too unique to be determined by the tribunal alone. This dragon's presence, along with these two *citizens* of mine, has affected the greater human population of Multnomah, which falls under my care

---

[2] A Least weasel's lifespan is 1-2 years

and *protection*," he emphasized a few choice words and raised an eyebrow to see if the tribunal understood his implication. The tribunal heard the tone and stirred in their seats. Even the spirit of Crittenden was swirling about in indecision. Mayor Flint leaned down to Brant conspiratorially and whispered, "Plus, it's an election year, and I need the optics of a dragon in our city under my belt," as he winked at the two men. They drew back from him, clear disgust on their faces. Ms. Marguerita had buried her head in her hands and was shaking it back and forth in disbelief.

Still, Nico thought, *despite the spectacle he is making, it affords us a way out of the judgment, and any chance is a welcome one. Ms. Marguerita's hands are clearly tied, or she would have said something by now*. He looked at Brant and saw the same thoughts written on his face.

Brant stood with the mayor, saying, "Yes, it can't be fair for the judgment to only fall to magickind. The burden of the decision should be made with a human on the panel as well." He didn't like what the mayor might come up with, but at this point, he just wanted a way out of this clearing.

"Exactly!" said Mayor Flint. "Gus should be brought before the public, before our human judge, and of course, the tribunal may be in attendance, as well," he waved dismissively. The tribunal's expression turned thunderous, but they said nothing.

Brant and Nico waited for the panel to protest and insist on their control over this decision, but a complicated series of expressions crossed their faces. The vampire woman looked thoroughly displeased as she had stood when the mayor began speaking and paced back and forth in front of their assembly. She looked as if she were ready to pounce at the smallest word. The pixie and the werewolf were deep in conversation, frowning and shaking their heads. The spirit of Crittenden was swirling about, rising in the air as though she wanted to vanish.

The mayor spoke again, leaning against the table Brant, Nico, and Ms. Marguerita sat at, almost absent-mindedly straightening his tie and brushing non-existent dust from his shoulder.

"You know I'm right about this, folks. Not even your dwarven kin or the centaurs showed their faces tonight. I wonder why they didn't want to risk the...arrangement we have," he spoke smoothly, but there was a palpable knife edge underneath it.

What is he talking about? Nico thought frantically. He, like Brant, just wanted to get Gus out of the situation. He had never liked the idea of the tribunal to begin with, but things could go from bad to worse. It's true, there was no human representative here, other than Ms. Marguerita. And there was no magical foster family present, either. Was this tribunal all a farce to try to capture Gus? Nico was growing more alarmed by the second, and he could see Brant was done with this whole entanglement also. Magickind certainly had their own rules and inner workings, and those were hard enough to understand what was at stake, but now there were human politics to contend with, as well?

This last sentiment spoken by the mayor was the final straw, and the pixie looked sharply at him. Despite her wariness at the evident warning in his tone, she flicked her wrist and the rangers just...appeared, swarming all around them. They stood to the side of each tribunal member, tall entities in dark brown, hooded cloaks. They each carried a black staff made of petrified wood and a leather pouch at their waist. In unison, they all took two steps forward, widening their stance, forming a linked-arm wall in front of the tribunal.

The mayor waved his hands in a gesture of reconciliation. "Yes, yes, I understand. Let the conversation continue in the lifespan of —" one of his bodyguards spoke quietly in his ear again, "a silkworm moth.[3] We will have an assembly prepared." He turned to the humans, giving his fake political smile and parade wave. He backed out of the clearing, the sarcasm evident as he sneered, "Partings."

Sparing a quick glance at Ms. Marguerita, Brant saw her nod wearily, waving a hand at them to go. So Brant, Nico, and Gus wasted no time hurrying out of the clearing, winding their way quickly through the market and back out into the relative safety of the human world.

---

[3] A Silkworm moth's lifespan is 3-5 days

CHAPTER 18

June 23rd

The next morning Brant and Nico called an emergency meeting of all the recruits who were in town, along with Koffe and Paula. There were too many people, though, and not everyone could fit in the carport, garage, and house, so they split the meeting into four sessions that day at 9 a.m., 12 p.m., 3 p.m., and 6 p.m. Oded stayed the whole day to support Brant, who was a bit frazzled. Before the morning meeting had started, however, the mayor's office called.

"Hello, you two! I hope you had a good night's sleep after you left," Mayor Flint said cheerily when Brant answered the phone.

"What do you want?" Brant said, dispensing the niceties and getting straight to the point. They hadn't seen the mayor since the dramatic exit the night before. Brant put the call on speakerphone so Nico and Oded could listen in. Koffe and Paula were nearby in the living room and came over, also.

Nico raised his eyebrows at Brant's brusque response but said nothing. He often saw his friend use bravado when respect was more called for, but he also knew that Brant saw layers of intention that he couldn't detect. If Brant thought the mayor was playing some unseen game beyond what the politician had stated last night, addressing it head-on would be best. They didn't know how much time they had, so every precious moment mattered.

You could nearly taste the oily texture of the words the mayor spoke next. "Want? It's not about what *I* want. It's about what this city *needs*. And we need to know that a big, strong dragon is going to protect us from the vampires, werewolves, and anything else that goes bump in the night to scare the fine citizens of Multnomah." The mayor's words sounded almost genuine if not for the affected tone of fake concern that came in at the end.

Brant gritted his teeth and counted to three, mouthing the numbers silently as he took deep breaths.

"I don't know what sort of leverage you have with the tribunal, but Gus. is not. a pawn. for your political career." Brant said with relative calm, given the steely glint in his eyes.

The mayor paused and sighed with disappointment, clicking his tongue.

"Listen. We are in a unique situation, you and I," Brant rolled his eyes at the mayor's attempt to cajole him. Mayor Flint continued, "I meant what I said last night at the town hall. Magickind aren't the only ones affected by Gus. Citizens have been calling me for weeks, flooding my office with letters, appointments, and phone calls. The pressure is mounting, and we have to figure out the next steps. Is Gus a threat? An asset? Do we need a yearly festival? Sacrifices? Heck, I don't know. Work with me here."

Brant's face showed a complicated range of emotions. He looked at Nico, and Nico shook his head in frustrated despair. *Why could no one just accept Gus's presence and let xer live?* Nico thought.

Brant replied in a reserved tone. "What do you have in mind, exactly?"

The mayor sighed, this time with triumphant relief. He continued in barely controlled excitement, "I am making arrangements for Black Bear Stadium to assemble a podium and a panel. Our magical ambassadors will be there, of course, but there will also be the historian and a circuit court judge. And I will be there to guide the proceedings," he said, the joy clear in his voice.

"We will discuss it with Gus and get back to you," Brant said in a clipped tone. "Subjecting Gus to more judgment and scrutiny is not in xer's best interest."

"What's in *your* best interest, frankly, is to let the public see Gus and determine for themselves if they feel safe. I can either sway them in your favor or... against," he said the last word so casually, almost off-hand, but you could hear the implication that he held the power of their lives in his hands. The mayor was making his message plain: work with him or he could — and would — make their lives a nightmare.

It's like being caught between the civil serpent and the stormy sea, Brant reflected. They either face the judgment of the tribunal and risk never seeing Gus again or face the manipulations of the mayor trying to curry favor for his election campaign. The mayor would probably try, at best, parading Gus like a prize, or at worst, Gus is chased out of town. *Come to think of it*, Brant realized, *It won't come to that. Gus would go back into hibernation rather than risk human lives.*

"So what do you say, young man?" the mayor said, breaking Brant out of his reverie. He looked around at everyone assembled. He considered Gus, who was sleeping in the basement, cuddled up with a tattered bee plushie. Xer had outgrown the house. Things had come to a head and there was no denying that they could make these decisions on their own.

"We'll be there. Let us know when," Brant said heavily, putting down the phone as if it were a 20-pound weight.

Before anyone could say anything, Brant walked out the front door and addressed the crowd across the street that had been there for months. He had never interacted with them directly before, but he looked across them all now, and a hush fell over the onlookers.

Brant spoke in a loud voice that carried across the crowd and could be heard down the street. He was angry and sad, but mostly, he felt resigned.

"The mayor is calling for a town viewing at the stadium in a few days. You can all voice your concerns at that time. There's no need to wait here to see something, say something, or act on something. Go to the stadium, get seats, and call the mayor's office for the details. You will never get what you want out here."

He turned away before anyone could respond and trudged back into the house.

As he walked back in through the front door, Brant could see that Nico, Oded, Koffe, and Paula were all waiting for him in the living room, talking quietly amongst themselves. They held steaming mugs of coffee or tea in front of them, and plates of pastries from the larder that Brant always had stocked. He was grateful to his past-self for preparing goodies. It was the oil in the chaos engine that had become his life, and he thanked the heavens for the millionth time for the comfort that baking brought him, both in the making and in the resulting enjoyment.

Brant sat down heavily in the armchair, looking up at Nico, finally.

Nico's face was drawn, full of grief, but also acceptance. He said quietly to Brant, "It's time."

Nico went downstairs to rouse Gus when he heard the chime from his phone that someone was at the side door. He was just climbing the stairs when he saw Ms. Marguerita nod at him as she made her way into the living room. As the ambassador to the tribunal, it made sense that she was here to follow up after the town hall. Nico dreaded that she might yell at them about how it had gone, but her face was inscrutable, and she said nothing.

Brant gave Ms. Marguerita the armchair while he pulled a spare seat from the dining room. Gus padded in but sat with a tall posture facing into the room, eyes alert. Xer glanced back and forth between Nico and Brant. Gus seemed to be scanning the two of them. With closed eyes, xer bowed xer's head down as if the news were a weight on xer's neck.

I will not go to this gathering, Gus mind-spoke to Nico and Brant. Ms. Marguerita looked sharply at Gus, and Brant realized that she could hear Gus, as well. *How interesting,* thought Brant to himself, *but not that surprising. She has secrets, that one.*

The direct voice of Gus in their heads wasn't comfortable, nor was it pleasurable, either. It was like wearing a bad pair of headphones in a crowded airport. You could hear the conversational crowd, but also the layers of crackling music.

I need to find my kin. I will soon complete the last stage of transformation and cannot remain here. I am not bound by human law or the laws of younger magickind. I was here long before the first of them were ever dreamed of. I am beholden to none but dragonkind, laws kept secret from humans. I am a sentient being with rights of dignity and honor, and a contributing member of the civilized world. I have seen persecution time and time again among humans. I only woke from the stone to see if you had returned to accepting each other as equals. There's been no indication of direct diplomacy, only pressure to conform, aggression to submit, and fear.

I will not stay where I am not fully accepted. I thought the time of inclusion was now; it is why I returned. But I can see it was folly.

You have given me shelter, love, kindness — there was a pause and Gus's mindvoice took on a wry tone, *cheesy puffs of air. You have done your best and I am grateful. You are both welcome on my journey.*

"Wait!" cried Nico aloud as Gus turned to go back downstairs. Paula, Oded, and Koffe looked around in confusion. They couldn't hear Gus in their minds. Only a few seconds had passed, and suddenly Nico was on his feet.

"I need you here," he said, throwing his arms around Gus's shoulders. Gus bowed xer's head and nudged Nico away, ever so gently.

You have blossoms everywhere, Gardener. I must find mine. Come with or stay, but I am going.

Brant had also stood and was looking at Gus, a question in his eyes.

"When?" was all he said in a strangled tone. He looked seconds away from breaking down himself. Oded looked pained when he saw Brant struggling to keep his composure. He came and stood next to him, placing his hand on his back in gentle support.

I will meet you after the human gathering, Gus answered him, and turned away, moving back downstairs silently, *to get your answer.*

The next two days were a blur as the house was a train station of visitors, debriefings, confusion, and concern in the house. Paula, Koffe, and Oded had all been brought up to speed on Gus's decision and helped to disseminate the latest news to all of those Gus had brought to town. Gus did not resurface during this time, refusing to even eat the offerings brought to xer. Gus stayed in a kind of alert meditation, occasionally pulsing out xer's deep, bone-rattling sonic waves for just a few seconds. Nico and Brant had huddled in Brant's room for hours, talking over whether they wanted to risk the wrath of the tribunal and the mayor by refusing to attend the stadium gathering, or if they wanted to go with Gus to wherever xer was headed.

They considered whether they had anything of value to offer Gus on xer's travels. What was the right choice? Ultimately, Multnomah was their home. It was where their jobs and families were, and their new budding relationships. Not to mention all the new people that Gus had introduced them to. Would any of those new residents stay if Gus wasn't here? And how would they pull off an extended trip, given how many people were demanding answers? Could they even get Gus out of town without being seen and stopped? Who could stop Gus, and how might they do it if they tried? How was Gus planning to travel unseen?

There were a million questions and no time to dig for answers.

In between the meetings, Brant's old detective buddy came by to talk about the buzz on the street from the mayor's office. The detective confirmed that the mayor was pulling out all the stops; he had been running radio and television ads for hours, encouraging people to get tickets to the stadium to "be heard" about the presence of a dragon in Multnomah. He arrogantly thought of himself as some sort of ringmaster, and it disgusted Brant and Nico that they had at least one more encounter with the man and his love of pageantry.

Ms. Marguerita had suggested that several of the people that Gus had attracted to town come to the stadium to give testimony on their behalf. In the past, she had been a bit circumspect, but Brant and Nico trusted that she truly did have Gus's welfare in mind when it came to her actions.

That mysterious quality was present even at the end because as she paused in the doorway to leave, she spent a long moment staring at the entry to the basement, still in its raw frame from when they had to extract Gus from the jambs. She turned to Nico, and patted his cheek affectionately, saying softly, "I will see you at the third."

Then she walked briskly out, her heavy jewelry making small tinkling noises that faded under her clicking heels hitting the sidewalk.

Brant turned to Nico. "What was that about?" he said, puzzled.

"I wish I knew," Nico said, baffled.

Gus has been so restless at night, and now I know why. I'll bet the yearning for family must've been very painful while this whole circus has gone on.

We have failed Gus, and we have to make it right.

Chapter 19

June 26th

After three days of weighing the pros and cons of leaving with Gus, it was the day of the stadium gathering. The mayor tried to send a van for Gus's transport, but Brant and Nico refused, preferring instead to use Koffe's van. They had decided to hold off on revealing that Gus wouldn't be there until they were at the public viewing. They knew that this was a major risk and that some of the people — especially the mayor — would be angry, but it was the last thing they could both do to protect Gustopher. No matter what the reception would be and no matter their future, Brant and Nico both wanted Gus to have the best and happiest life possible since coming out of hibernation.

As they drove to Black Bear Stadium on the other side of the river, there was silence in the van. It was early evening, but the sun was still high in the sky, beaming its cheerful rays across the glittering waters of the Whilamut River. There was the usual flurry of activity at the waterfront when the weather was nice: bicyclists, walkers, dogs on leashes, kids playing in the iconic Old Town fountain. Even a unicyclist or two was practicing. Nico glanced back at the cargo area, all of the dread and fears of the last few months swirling in his heart like the first tendrils of a tornado as he recalled that Gus had sat there only a few nights before. He was terrified of standing in front of a crowd, trying to explain and justify why Gus had every right to exist and live among all the other species on Earth. Why was this so hard for people to understand?

Brant held a stony clench to his jaw as he navigated the city streets, but his distracted expression showed he was working through what to say in front of the gathered masses. He had the same look as when the lieutenant colonel had first showed up at their door: closed but calculating. Nico was grateful his friend was a better speaker in times of crisis. He couldn't believe it hadn't even been a year he had known this man. He honestly couldn't picture a future in which he and Gus and Brant weren't all together. It was what had made the last few days so difficult.

He knew Gustopher could take care of xerself. He also knew that Gus couldn't remain at the house. He knew that he should continue fostering the connections with Bisan, his family, and the new friendships that had been forged because of Gus. But in his heart, there was only one road forward, no matter how many unknowns there were. No matter how many opportunities he might miss. As he stared thoughtfully out the window, he made his decision about whether or not to stay.

Brant glanced at Nico, studying him for a moment, frowning, but said nothing as they pulled into the loading dock area.

In order to fool the mayor and the security staff as long as possible, several of the new allies had worked with Terri the magician to build a papier-mâché dragon inside of a cage to sell the illusion until the big reveal. They would keep the cage covered until the mayor made them remove it. It was Brant's idea to, "Trojan Horse this bullshit rodeo," as he had put it so colorfully a few nights prior. He reasoned that if the mayor was going to put on a spectacle, so would they.

Brant was in a particularly ornery mood as they pulled in. He'd even had a giant red button made so he could pin it to his shirt that read in block, white letters, "Hello! My kid's pronouns are xer/xers." He had mentioned that he had another surprise in store but wanted to keep it from Nico until the "right moment." Nico felt a little current of dread on top of his crushing anxiety, but he had to admit that Brant's schemes did usually turn out well.

Black Bear Stadium was the local hub for sporting events, music festivals, ceremonies of state, and historical celebrations. It had an open-air rooftop with rigging that allowed a cover to go out over the field and cover the participants from the perpetual rain. Being built as a modular unit meant that seats could be cordoned off for better safety and crowd control for smaller events, such as this one. The stadium could hold up to 50,000 people, but today the staff had prepared the walkways, parking, seating, and refreshments for 20,000. Even from where they were deep in the bowels of the stadium, Nico could hear the throngs so well that he could picture all of those seats totally filled.

As they were unloading the cage onto flat carts with wheels, Nico could see a glimpse through one of the passageways that led out onto the field. The walkway was so wide that two cars could've easily driven through it and not touched each other. He could see several thousand from his vantage point, and there was a palpable tone of excitement in the air as people talked, laughed, held signs, and shouted with impatience. Nico's heart dropped to his stomach. He wondered if the people who had been camped on his street for the last several months were out there, and what they would say. This many people made his brain turn to white noise as he froze in place.

Brant came over and gave Nico a small shake on the shoulder.

"Hey, man. It's going to be okay. We got this," he reassured Nico. "This is all going to work out," Brant paused, looking down at the floor and mumbled softly. "I know you've decided to go. I want you to know, I've decided too. I am not going back to a life without Gus. I've already found the peace I needed after coming home. I can rebuild that anywhere. If you are going with Gus, I'm coming along."

Nico looked at his friend, a frown of concern evident in his eyes. "Are you sure? You are the one who has the most to leave behind. And we don't even know where we are going."

Brant smiled defiantly, and Nico recognized the manic gleam in his eye. "Like I said, dude. You go, xer goes, I am there, too."

Nico grinned back, his heart swelling with more love than he'd ever known, tamping down the terror of facing the public. He soaked up the chaos, love, and kinship in those words.

"Let's go blow some minds before we hit the road, then," Nico said, turning back to the van. After a pause, he said, almost just to himself, "Big day."

He could hear Brant's faint response as he walked to the other side of the van.

"Big damn day."

As they wheeled out the covered cage onto the ramp that lay across the clipped Astroturf, Nico surveyed the gathered crowd. Despite the fact that the stadium wasn't full, the sheer volume of this many people talking, laughing, and cheering was unreal. Nico felt as if he were standing next to an airplane engine as compared to his usual days at the gardens. He felt obliterated by the noise, burst out of solid form, and scattered to the winds. He thought he caught a shimmer out of the corner of his eyes and felt a quick gust of wind, but when he looked behind him, nothing was there.

Brant glanced over and reached into his pocket. He handed Nico a sealed packet of earplugs and Nico nodded gratefully. After a few moments with the unrelenting sound deadened, Nico could breathe a sigh of relief. Having a best friend was a feeling like nothing else on Earth. They just understood you better than you knew yourself.

Brant crooked a smirk and pushed the cage up the ramp to the raised platform, pretending to strain from the effort. Nico ducked his head so no one would see him smile at his friend's antics.

Mayor Fraco Flint stood near a podium, pacing back and forth and strutting about like a sage grouse, arching his neck and puffing out his chest. He was visibly impatient and enjoying all the attention. A gleam came into his eye when he saw Brant and Nico come up the ramp with the presumed dragon. Nico felt a thrill of rebellion, knowing that Mayor Flint's smug expression would soon be falling off his face.

The sun was still bright in the summer sky but had fallen behind the stadium walls, giving plenty of shade across the field. The raised platform had been placed in the center so that citizens could see it at the best possible vantage from the three sections that held open seats. Both the northern and southern sections were half full of about 5,000 people, but the bulk of them were in the western section, which filled nearly all of the 12,000 seats available.

The opening in the roof was a wide, clear rectangle as the retractable doors were tucked neatly under the roof frame, and a cool breeze drifted down the platform. The mayor imperiously directed Brant and Nico to roll the cage to the center, just behind his podium. They obliged and stepped to either side of the cage in preparation for the mayor's speech.

The crowd's swell of anticipation was palpable, and Nico felt sick. He took steadying breaths, trying to remain calm as he surveyed the tribunal flanking him and Brant in raised chairs on each side of the podium. Ms. Marguerita was there next to the circuit court judge in a black robe. The judge was a stern-faced woman with high bouffant hair sprayed like a raised helmet. Her hair reminded Nico of a 1970s real estate agent. Ms. Marguerita gave him an encouraging smile and he nodded back at her in the same way he had seen at the night market. She smiled bigger in return.

Mayor Flint checked his watch and tapped the microphone importantly.

He cleared his throat and the crowd fell quiet. It was eerie for Nico, but he took out his earplugs to better hear the mayor.

Brant watched the idiot mayor walk about with all the arrogance and ignorance of a fraternity bro at an astrophysics conference who had just asked about what his Pluto rising meant for his future. He hated that this man thought he had the two of them in his pocket. Nothing could be further from the truth. He relished what was about to unfold. There was nothing that made Brant more rebellious now than someone telling him what to do with his life. Those days were over, and his new journey with Gus and Nico — and even Oded — were where his sights were set. He was looking forward, and refusing to get pulled into political squabbles, night market blackmail, or giving in to military or science groups who wanted to lock Gustopher in a lab and experiment on xer. *Over my dead body*, thought Brant bitterly. He had cashed in a favor that was sure to add a little chaos to the proceedings, and if he wasn't mistaken, they should be showing up right in the middle of the mayor's speech.

The mayor had been talking for a few minutes now, trying to warm up the crowd with typical vague phrasings like, "for the greater good" and "in our best collective interest." Brant wasn't really listening, because he was busy assessing the crowd. There were definite pockets of those who were worried and fearful, their eyes darting back and forth from the mayor's face to the cage. But the majority of the crowd, surprisingly, was reflecting how Brant felt. Their faces were stony with mistrust and disrespect. Several of them were shaking their heads in frustration. The mayor ignored them and blithely carried on with his speech. As Brant cocked his ears to the entrance they had come in, he could hear the distant sound of motorcycles and he smiled genuinely with satisfaction. The shit show was about to begin.

Nico saw the mayor falter as he heard the motorcycles approaching, growing louder and louder as they rode out of the passageway from the lower levels of the stadium. The roar of about 30 engines gunning and revving grew thunderous as they spilled out onto the field, making circles and patterns impossible to follow. It reminded Nico of a burst of marbles across a tiled floor, a riot of noise and color. He glanced at

Brant peeking at him from the corner of the cage and saw a satisfied smirk at the corner of his friend's mouth. This must be the surprise he had in store. Nico shook his head in exasperation but said nothing. He couldn't; it was too much cacophony.

This wasn't just any motorcycle gang; these were the Titans. They were known for their volunteer work with domestic abuse victims, often sheltering them bodily when victims were fleeing their homes or blocking abusers with their bikes from pursuing. They had a hotline that anyone could call day or night if they needed physical protection or an escort service to safety. They often worked with homeless youth, displaced immigrants, and children from abusive homes. While they had a fierce appearance, they were known to be fair and always fighting on behalf of the underdog. Many of their members were trained in CPR, de-escalation techniques, and suicide prevention.

More importantly, they were beloved by the City of Multnomah. They had been around for over 40 years, serving the community and helping out those most desperate. They had earned the social clout the mayor so desperately craved and couldn't claim for himself. Nico watched as the mayor literally quivered at the ruckus they caused as they pulled up all around the platform, idling their engines like the growl of 20 jungle cats about to pounce.

Nico watched as Brant strode confidently over to the podium, taking the mic gently from the mayor while he was distracted, patting him on the back as if he'd planned it this way all along. The mayor quailed and shrunk back, trying to recover his authority by standing stiffly nearby.

Brant spoke to the gathered crowd, who had begun shifting uneasily.

"Hello to all of you. I realize you have come a long way to share your thoughts and concerns over the new magical resident of Multnomah. I'm sure some of you took time away from work and loved ones to be here. After all, it's a big moment, right?"

Several people nodded their heads in agreement.

Brant continued, "A dragon has not been seen for many hundreds of years, and I'm sure you must be curious as to what Gustopher looks like, and more importantly, what xer can do. Well, let's end the wait, shall we?" Brant paused to unhook the mic from the podium, walk back over to his spot, and grasp the corner of the fabric on his side of the cage. He held the mic down at his side, and nodding in time with Nico as they whisper-counted down to three, they unveiled the cage in one dramatic motion.

CHAPTER 20

Sitting inside the cage sat a crude, papier-mâché dragon about five feet high. It did have somewhat of xer's likeness, as it had Gus's mismatched eyes and goofy grin. It had no prowess or gravitas, of course, which was the point. Brant studied the crowd and did see a few outraged faces, but he also saw amusement and satisfaction as well. He raised the mic and addressed the crowd.

"Yes, this is a bit of a trick. Gustopher is not really here. This was the only way to get you and the mayor's attention long enough to listen to us," Brant scowled at the mayor, who had the sense to look abashed. Brant continued, his tone back to compassionate and brisk. Ms. Marguerita wore a bigger smile than Nico had ever seen on the old Italian's face.

"No one has granted *us* the opportunity to speak, and we needed this moment to help you understand. Gustopher is a sentient and highly intelligent *individual* who is fully self-sufficient. Gus communicates telepathically and with visions, which we've both experienced firsthand. Gus has been sharing with us for many months now about xer's identity, needs, and desires. While we can understand that you might feel threatened, Gus poses *no harm to the citizens of Multnomah,* human or magical. Gus feels so strongly about this, as well as xer's freedom and right to exist peaceably, that xer has left," Brant finished abruptly, struggling to keep his composure. He looked over at Nico for support, who nodded solemnly in encouragement.

Brant swallowed and heard the murmurings of the crowd as they absorbed this news. He raised the mic again. "Gustopher is a very, very old individual and does not consent to scrutiny," Brant paused at each of these words, looking at Lieutenant-Colonel Hatworth, "experimentation," Brant looked at Dr. LaBorn, "judgment," Brant glared at the tribunal, and finally turned, pointedly looking to the mayor, "or wants to participate in leveraging anyone's ambitions."

Nico felt as if his heart might burst with the sheer defiant happiness he felt at witnessing Brant's composed outrage and blatant protection of Gustopher. He wished Gus were here to witness this. He turned back to see the crowd's reaction. Brant wasted no time by addressing them again.

"In the stands with you are several people who have been drawn to our town by Gus's magics. They will share with you their experiences and give testimony as to xer's personality and living habits. You start first, Koffe."

In the seats, Koffe stood with a portable mic and addressed the crowd all around him. As he spoke of Gus when they had first met, you could see the people near him delighted in the stories of baby Gus, tearing into drawers, sleeping with xer's mouth open, and making tiny roars when xer didn't get what xer wanted. Next was Paula, Koda, Cecilia, Hermengildo. Then Laszlo, Koker, Charles, Terri, Sylvester. Nico could even make out Bisan, and his heart beat fast at seeing her warm smile among so many strangers. The mic was passed to Oded next, Neil, Sawyer.... and more, and more. There were at least four or five allies in every seating section, and while they didn't talk long, and nearly all of them were nervous, they all had positive things to say about Gus, reiterating over and over that xer was not a threat.

Nico swayed a little, unsteady and shocked at all the evident support and commitment everyone had for Gus, some of whom had only known xer for a few weeks. Tears came to his eyes as his own father stood and spoke on behalf of Nico and Brant, praising them both for raising Gus in an environment that was safe for humans during Gus's growth. *He basically raised us, but let's not split hairs,* Nico thought, chuckling to himself under his breath.

As the testimonials came to a close, a tall person to the left of the podium waved to Brant frantically, and Brant motioned them to come down and address the microphone that had been set up for questions. As the tall stranger made their way down the aisle, Nico could make out the rainbow pride flag everywhere on their clothing; it was on their sleeves, their pants, their giant sunhat, and they had alternating blue and pink long hair that fell to their shoulders. They teetered over to the mic on rainbow platform boots covered in sequins. Nico thought they looked vaguely familiar but couldn't place their face.

This bright soul made their way to the mic, saying breathlessly, "Oh my gosh, hello to the beautiful souls of Multnomah! What a gift to be here and to meet Gus's daddies. So handsome too, am I right?" they said coquettishly, a little flirt in their question as they winked at Brant. Brant looked flattered and winked back.

"Oh la la! What a hunk. Okay, so my name is Mercury Novalux and I help run the local LGBTQIA+ nonprofit organization called Multi-Pride, for Multnomah and multiple types of gay pride, get it? Anyway. We've been hearing about Gus for months now and thought that a show of support was way overdue. So darlings, we just wanted to thank you two papas and your crew for all of these testimonials and thank the mayor as well for orchestrating this," Mercury winked and waved at the mayor, who instinctively waved back, "but there's really no need for alarm, pumpkin butts, because we already claim Gus as one of our own."

Brant's face darkened slightly, and he asked Mercury with an arched eyebrow, "One of *your* own?"

"Oh dear! No, I said that wrong. Let me try again, you spicy tart. We are here to bear witness to what Gus decides for *xerself*, and accept whatever decision Gus makes, again, for *xerself*. We have a bit of experience with the right to life, liberty, and the pursuit of happiness, you know." Mercury paused at this and turned back to the crowd, raising their hand high in the air.

At this, nearly 80% of the crowd stood, cheering, some holding signs over their heads reading:

"We accept you, Gus!"

"Be the Gus you want to see in the world!"

"Gustastic!"

and "Gus, the gender-free dragon!"

Mercury turned back to the microphone and addressed the mayor with a mischievous smile. "If the mayor thinks that we residents are going to stand by while he tries to instigate fear and hysteria about the beloved Gus, *we will. vote him. out. of. office,*" they concluded firmly, but with great cheer.

A chant had started in the crowd of "Stop the Fear, Stop the Hate! Stop the Fear, Stop the Hate!"

Brant waved his hands for quiet, and the crowd fell to an immediate hush. The silence happened so quickly and so suddenly, he realized it couldn't have been him that they were responding to. With a thrill in his throat, *It would be just like Gus to* — he thought, turning to Nico, who had also turned and was looking behind him.

There, just beyond the platform, standing regally in the fake grass and surrounded by gaping Titan motorcyclists, towering as tall as an elephant, was Gustopher.

Chapter 21

I need to see for myself, see what my kin was subjecting themselves to on my behalf. It had been hundreds of years of waiting, always waiting, for the humans to realize how powerful and important togetherness is. I have grown bitter and closed off in my heart after seeing the fear of the unknown — of me — only as a...thing that is new to their world, the place they think they own and possess. I am leaving to protect them as much as myself. It is time for me to find others of my kind and to release my human friends from the burden that my presence was causing.

As soon as they left the house, I flew to a remote region in the mountains to complete my transformation, keeping low to the trees and using my illusion magic. A highly useful skill, and the slowest to return to me during the transition stage. A clearing of trees was the perfect location for my magics to unleash. In the soft pine leaves I shiver and rumble, letting out another of my sonic messages to the other dragons. This is a tightly guarded secret that the humans must not know, as it is evident from the uniformed man that they would find a way to stifle it, to control and suppress it. Our sonic signals are how we find one another, how we bring each other out of hibernation. I have been sending out messages as I grew stronger. I can only hope that one of my kind hears the call.

It doesn't take long for my full-size wings and long-scaled tail to reach their full size. My claws have thickened and grown stronger. My back is wider, my shoulders ache with power and muscles kept small and disused. My head and snout are longer, my ears now fully match my frame. My scales lie flat, a thick but smooth, dark pearlescent green that matches the trees. Only a few grey freckles remain from my time as stone. I am starved from the effort and find several birds to stalk and sneak up on, even an injured hawk. I find a stream to drink from, and though there are no decadent human foods here, it will suffice.

I stretch my wings and take to the sky again, soaring higher than I have in 400 years. I nearly cry out with ecstasy after months of being inside, recuperating and growing stronger. I pull my illusion magic tight around my body, bending light so that no one can see me against the blue of the radiant sky. I dive a few times, stretching my wings and feeling the ripple of the undercurrent flutter beneath my outstretched limbs. By the winds, there is nothing on this Earth like flying. What a gift, is this life.

I must see them one last time. They will not know of my presence, even the younger magical ones. I fly west, picking up speed as I sense the gardener's mind. He is the closest to me now in spirit. He comprehends more than the others, except the small woman with the big adornments. She is savvy, that one. She is connected, like the gardener is to me.

I have found them all, my noble kin. They are out in the open, defending me before a crowd. The bossy one is speaking. I dive down into the stadium's open roof and land silently, crouching low so that no one may hear me. My heart clenches in fear, is this like before? Will the crowd hurt them, throw stones? Cast them out in banishment? I cannot let this happen again. They may not accept dragons, but my human family will not suffer for it. I made mistakes before; I did not use my power. I thought diplomacy would prevail.

But now... no. Now I will show them they cannot persecute.

As I start to rise, I hear voices from the crowd. It is my allies, those whom I've attracted with my affinity. Their voices carry some sort of incantation magic across the gathering so that all may hear. They are so magnificently different from each other, bringing new points of view, beautiful in their collective knowledge and wisdom, humor and talents. They are speaking of me, now, what is this? They are swaying the crowd, giving testimony to dragonkind. Okay, so the music man did not have to mention my weakness for cheese puffs. Rude.

Now this rainbow-colored person approaches the special stick. Is this the same magic? Their voice carries wide, and I can see people rising. Here it is, this is the persecution. I stand, ready to react. The fire in my throat burns, ready to lay waste.

Wait.

What is this feeling...

They speak of acceptance.

A tentative wave of relief touches my heart.

They care about my freedom.

A second wave, stronger, laps insistently at my heart's bitter shores.

They are fierce about my inherent right of existence.

A tidal wave of emotion, crashing over my burning throat, leaving me stunned. They comprehend, they have transformed themselves. They have wisdom and grace in the face of the unknown.

Nico and Brant both walk over to Gus, ignoring the stunned silence of the crowd, the tribunal, the mayor, and the judge. Brant looks up and further up, finally catching Gus's eye.

Brant spoke in his signature conversational playfulness, "I see you've had a growth spurt."

Nico sighed a little dramatically for effect. "They grow up so fast, you know? Seems like just yesterday xer was yea high," he gestured at his waist, shaking his head in mock sorrow, but his eyes twinkled up at Gustopher.

Brant grinned at Nico, but addressed Gus, "You feeling okay, bud?"

Gus nodded xer's head solemnly, once.

"Did you have something you wanted to say, Gus?" Nico asked the dragon gently.

Gus nodded xer's head again, once. Xer nudged Nico closer to the podium. Nico looked hesitantly at Brant, but Brant replied, "Gus wants you to speak for xer. You can't say no. Sorry, bud. You can do it. I'll be right here. These Titans will cover our exit if we have to get out," he nodded encouragingly at Nico.

Nico approached the microphone, Gus thudding to the side of the platform because xer wouldn't fit with all the other humans crowded there.

The humans on the platform shifted uneasily in their seats, except, of course, Ms. Marguerita. She was beaming from ear to ear, her legs crossed casually, her hands clasped in nearly gleeful anticipation.

The crowd had been stirring but settled immediately. The quiet draped heavily onto Nico like a weighted blanket. He felt both trapped and comforted by it. His eyes sought the faces he had come to know in the last few months, and they gave him courage. He closed his eyes and took a few steadying breaths. The crowd waited so quietly you could hear a leaf drop.

Then, clear and liquid-smooth in Nico's mind, he could hear Gus.

For the last 400 years, there has been only pressure to conform, an aggression for us to submit, and so much fear. Until today. I accept the welcome of the rainbow ones. I have seen many centuries where paranoia and banishment have driven the minds of humans, and even that of magickind.

I will return to this region when my search is complete.

Nico relayed Gus's message word for word, his voice shaking a little in front of the crowd. He did not tell the public about the road trip as he and Brant had not discussed what they wanted to disclose to the mayor or the tribunal. He glanced at Ms. Marguerita and saw her nodding with approval at his discretion.

The crowd began a tentative clapping and cheering that grew louder as they processed what Gus had said through Nico. The cheers grew louder, and Gus even stood a little taller at the reception. You could see the crinkle of a smile at the corner of xer's mouth and after a quick iridescent ripple up xer's spine, Gus opened xer's mouth and let out a burst of warm yellow light into the sky.

The crowd gasped with shock, but quickly recovered and cheered for more.

Nico and Gus moved to the back of the platform to confer with Brant as the mayor tried to recover his position in front of the crowd. He had taken the mic again and was promoting the presence of Gus. He attributed the spike in economic prosperity for the last eight months to xer bringing new people to the city, and with it, a marked increase in small businesses, lower crime, and more housing sales. The crowd cheered at this, but it was clear that the main event was over. The stands started to empty as people began to leave.

Nico turned to Gus as the crowd was dispersing. "I am coming with you. I don't know where we are going, and it will be hard on my family, but I can come back. This is important. I want to be there, to see what you find and help other humans understand."

Brant nodded in agreement. "What he said. By the way, that's some cool talent you got there, going totally invisible? I take it you don't pass out now?"

Gus shook xer's head, no.

"You have many skills, Gus," Brant said, shaking his head ruefully.

If there was a dragon talent show, I would win.

Brant replied out loud, "You, like all children, have watched entirely too much television." He paused briefly, considering the idea.

"Dragon talent show," he muttered. "That's just what we need."

CHAPTER 22

June 26th Late Evening

Brant and Nico headed home to pack up and make arrangements. Before they were dashing off, however, there were a few pressing matters to take care of before they were going to meet Gus at the outskirts of town. They also both wanted to leave before the squabbling of the different factions began jockeying for endless meetings, requesting assurances they couldn't give. It was a good start, but it was still just a start, and they needed time away from the pressure of the last several months.

Nico called Bisan and asked if she could meet urgently, and she readily agreed. She sounded as if she was expecting his call. He gave her the address of a cafe near his house.

She sat staring out the window when he walked in. She was at a table with her legs neatly tucked under, her hands hovering over a cup of hot coffee. As he arrived, she dropped a spoon she had been holding, and he bent quickly to retrieve it.

"Hi," Nico said softly.

"Hello yourself," Bisan replied, her eyes twinkling at him. His heart contracted a little, painful at the topic he needed to bring up,

"I don't have much time, but I wanted to see you. It's about Gus."

Bisan interrupted by holding up a hand, forestalling Nico. "Well, after meeting xer in person today — along with 12,000 other people, that is — I can see what all the fuss is about," she said wryly.

Nico snorted at the understatement. "Yeah, that last growth spurt was a doozy." He didn't have time, though, to ruminate on Gus's physical changes. He was worried he wouldn't be brave enough to say the next part, the part he absolutely needed to say.

"I'm leaving tonight. We are headed...somewhere, I don't know where. And I don't know exactly when we'll be back," he was looking down at his hands, clasped tightly on the table. "I understand if you want to —" Nico stopped abruptly when he felt his hands covered by hers, soft and still warm from holding the coffee. They had the slightest hint of cinnamon wafting up.

"You *are* coming back, though, yes?" she said, looking at him over their joined hands. Her voice was low, relaxed and intimate.

Nico said in reply, "Yes. My family is here. My home is here. I am coming back, no matter what." He studied her face, looking for some sign of rejection or anger. But there was just a serene smile, content and patient.

"Well, that's that, then. I will see you when you come back. But should you need someone to talk to, I'm happy to lend an ear. I'm sure your adventures are truly just beginning." Bisan loosened her hands and leaned back. She stood, grabbed her sweater from the back of the chair, and put her hand on his cheek, so, so gently. As Nico was looking up at her accepting and loving gaze, Bisan leaned down and kissed him.

It was tentative at first, but the longer they kissed, the desire rose in them both like a surging ocean wave. She leaned against Nico and his hands reached up, resting on her lower back. She broke away from the kiss, and, without a word, left him dazed in his chair. Nico spent a few minutes trying to get his mind to stop reeling and with a happy sigh, bounced out of the cafe and headed home to pack.

Several of the recruits were already there. The beauty of Gus's new matrix of allies meant that they weren't alone in this process and could share the numerous burdens among the many. There were people in town who had already settled in, ready to help manage the house and Brant's business. Communications were coming in every hour from friends of the network and friends of friends who were offering housing, cars, meals, clothes, whatever they needed. Word had spread so quickly that there was very little that Brant and Nico had to pack that was personal, as they would be well provided for along the way. Whatever that way was going to be.

The mayor's office had worked fast after the stadium gathering. Within hours, he had assembled a committee to address the question of Gus's legal rights. The Multi-Pride leader, Mercury, had astutely brought an international immigration lawyer, and the mayor and the tribunal were working together to deal with the question of dragonkind and their unique contributions to both the human and magical world. On the committee would be a representative of all the different factions: magical, human, a city official on behalf of the City of Multnomah, a science representative, a military representative, and of course, if consented to, Gus, as one of dragonkind.

Nico drafted a letter of resignation with a pang in his heart. He loved the gardens, and he would miss them. He was glad that he had several people who would be taking care of his bonsai collection at home, as well as looking after Brant's business.

He told Brant about his conversation with Bisan, and Brant patted him on the back in sympathy. Since both of them were dealing with the same unknowns as to when they would return, Nico knew that a conversation with Oded was coming, as well.

He watched as Brant walked over to the handsome musician, who was checking a first-aid kit for the car to make sure none of the supplies were expired. Oded read Brant's expression and nodded, and the two of them went back to Brant's bedroom and shut the door. Nico hoped for both of their sake that more answers would be coming soon. He knew it felt terrible for Bisan and Oded to be the ones waiting, but it was equally as bad to be the ones responsible for dangling vague promises without knowing whether or not they would be fulfilled.

Koffe had been generous enough to swap vehicles and he was taking Nico's SUV in exchange for the van, which could house them and their stuff more easily as they traveled. After all the instructions were laid out, phone numbers were swapped, maps were consulted, van was packed, and goodbyes were said, Brant and Nico both spent a few minutes looking at the house from the street.

"So, off into the great unknown."

"Yep."

"Want to go meet our cheeky little dragon friend?"

"I wish Gus was little again. Xer was so stinking cute."

"I could do with having cheese puffs to myself, you know."

"Forget it, dude. Those days are over."

Nico guided Brant through the winding road that grew more and more narrow into the mountains. The traffic was dense at first but grew less so the further they traveled. They had been driving for a little over an hour when Nico directed Brant to take a rural road that led deeper into the foothills, bouncing through the muddy tracts on the dirt road. Eventually they turned onto a logging road barely wider than a deer trail. Here they rolled down the windows, breathing in the still-crisp air of the shaded forest canopy.

They arrived at a clearing and parked the van. Sitting in the clearing was Gus, looking so at ease and happy, xer's wings fluttering lazily in the cool air.

Good. Now we can begin.

"What do you mean, Gus? Do you know where we are going?" Nico remarked anxiously. He had struggled on the drive with not knowing their destination, whereas Brant had handled it a bit better, taking a cavalier attitude. Brant asked, "What's Gus saying?"

Patience.

Gus closed xer's eyes and a few seconds passed. Then, Nico's phone rang in his pocket. He checked the caller I.D. and gasped. He looked at Brant while answering the phone, "Remi?!"

Brant had just started to say, "You tell that little —" but Nico waved him quiet as he put the vampire on speaker.

"Mai oui, of course, mon petit Faisselle! Have you missed me?" Remi sounded exactly the same, flippant and playful.

"Where have you been?! Why haven't you been answering my calls? We have SO much to share with you," Nico said in a rush, barely able to keep in the words.

"You think you are the only one getting visions, ma belle?" Remi clucked his tongue disapprovingly. "Silly young man."

"Wait —" started Nico, but Remi cut him off.

"There's simply no time, my scrumptious block of Mont Bleu. You must all come immediately to New Orleans."

Brant and Nico stared at each other as Remi dropped the final bombshell.

"The dragons are waking up."

Acknowledgements

None of this book would be possible without the support and love of my own chosen family and friends.

Special and outstanding recognition is due to everyone who donated to my fundraiser, but especially to Sierra Grace, Jackson Dickert, Joy Bandy, and Celeste Larson. And to my cat, Totoro, who worked the hardest of all. Just kidding; she did nothing. She didn't even take out the trash.

The team who helped me bring the story from marker-covered index cards written in the dead of night to elegant script is so talented in their own ways.

Those extraordinary humans are:

Developmental Editor, Sarah Faeth Sanders. Line and copy editor, Wendy Caesar. Sensitivity reader, Rina Amaranthine (@liquidrina). Beta readers: Stephanie Bjelland, Dietrich Stogner, Darcia Laucerica, Amy Wolford, Krista Smith, Anne Gearhart, Jessika Darkstar. Cover artist, Indiana Maria Acosta Hernandez, alias Indicreates. Typographer, Amphi Studio. Formatter, Painted Wings Publishing. Marketing, Morgan Evans.

This book was written via Campfire Writing. I used the Stanford Breath font for the cover and interior titles. To protect my intellectual property, I used Muso.com. I employed the outlining method, "Save The Cat." I used Portland, Oregon as inspiration for the region and city.

Several of my supporting characters are inspired by people in real life, most of whom I do not know at the time of this publication. I encourage you to look up their incredible projects.

- Bisan was inspired by the incredible civilian journalist, Bisan Owda, who has dedicated all of her heart and soul into amplifying the genocide of the Palestinian people. https://en.wikipedia.org/wiki/Bisan_Owda
- Ke Fuy Fukuhara was inspired by: https://en.wikipedia.org/wiki/Harry_K._Fukuhara
- Mercury Novalux was inspired by the incredible Trans Handy Ma'am, Mercury Stardust, who works tirelessly for the rights of marginalized people everywhere, but especially for the transgender community. https://mercurystardust.com/
- Michael LaBorn — who gave me explicit permission to use his full name in a not-very-nice character — is a champion of black and brown self-published authors. You can learn more about Michael's work at: https://www.tiktok.com/@michael.laborn
- Oded was inspired by a classical Indian musician, KabirCan'tSingh from TikTok. You can hear his music at: https://www.mehfilband.com/upcomingshows
- Sylvester Chakkalakal is inspired by a volunteer I saw who works for the nonprofit, FoodNotBombs in Houston, Texas, United States. You can find out more about them here — https://houstonfoodnotbombs.org/about/

Mayor Fraco Flint was modeled after the actor Cary Elwes' portrayal of Mayor Kline in the television show, *Stranger Things*.

Vico was so named in honor of Vico Ortiz, the genderfluid and nonbinary actor.

Laszlo was so named in honor of the incredible character in the television show, *What We Do in The Shadows*.

Neil was so named in honor of the writer, Neil Gaiman. (hi, Neil. Thanks for shaping the world to be a frighteningly fantastic gothic maze full of delight and suspense.)

Terri the magician was so named in honor of Sir Terry Pratchett.

Daddy Nyx was so named in honor of a close, personal friend of mine. You can find out more about her at Viridiluxconsulting.com.

Several characters in the book were so named because of people I've met in passing in real life who just had outstanding names. Ms. Marguerita C. Scarpelli, Koker F. Rathbone III, Cecilia Fullilove, Koda Sevltrywnak.

Lastly, Koffe is inspired by the name of my upstairs neighbor, who's a dad of 2 kids and just a sweet man. Fans of my writing know that this character was in my first book, *Stockings Required*, but didn't have a name and was just "Big Black Bouncer." He made his way into *Guarding Gus* as that same bouncer, but as far as I can tell, he's decided to continue and just show up in every book I write until I die.

Names & Pronunciations

People
Bisan — (Bee-sahn)
Bohunkus — (Boh-hunk-us)
Brant — (Brant)
Cecilia Fullilove — (See-sil-lia Full-i-luhv)
Cyr — (Sy-er)
Daddy Nyx — (Dad-di Nix)
Crittenden — (Crit-ten-dun)
Fraco Flint — (Fra-co Flint)
Gustopher — (Gus-tuh-fer)
Hermendgildo Garcia Angeles, Jr. — (Her-man-geel-do Garh-see-ya An-hel-es Joon-eyr)
Koker F. Rathbone III — (Coak-er Rath-bone)
Laszlo Toth — (Laz-lo Toth)
Koda Sevltrywnak — (Koda Sevel-triv-nack)
Ke Fuy Fukuhara — (Keh Foowi Fook-oo-hara)
Koffe — (Koh-feh)
Lezahtun — (Lays-ah-toon)
Malcolm Hatworth — (Mal-comb Hat-worth)
Marguerita Scarpelli — (Mar-ger-ita Scar-pelli)
Michael LaBorn — (Mi-kul La-born)
Mercury Novalux — (Mer-cure-ee)
Nico — (Nee-koh)
Oded — (O-ded)
Paula — (Paw-luh)
Remi — (Re-mee)
Sylvester Chakkalakal — (Sil-vest-er Chok-a-lock-al)
Silver — (Sil-ver)
Terri — (Ter-ree)
Sawyer — (Saw-yur)
Vico — (Vee-co)
Viscidius Rubra — (Vis-sid-ee-us Roo-bra)
Wali — (Wall-e)

Discussion Questions

There are several themes in *Guarding Gus* that continue to be explored in *What to Suspect When You're Suspecting*. These questions are meant to function as a guide among friends, family, and book clubs. Caution! There are spoilers ahead.

1. The question of Gustopher's rights continues to be a major theme of the book. Gus is an animal, but also sentient, able to communicate, and a member of a magical species. What parallels can you draw to non-domesticated animals in our world? What is the danger in having some exotic animals as pets?

2. Nico is misgendered twice, first by Brant and then by his father, Vico. Misgendering is a dehumanizing experience for trans people. What do you think about how each of them handled the conversation after? Is there something any of them might have done differently?

3. Nico's father pressures him to conform to Mexican family traditions. Latin culture is steeped in patriarchy. Vico's eventual acceptance of Nico is going to cause an impact for their family as a whole. Discuss this impact.

4. Gus is slow to regain xer's powers because of the outside pressures of politics, military, science representatives, and the general public. Do you think Gus would've grown faster if those external stressors not been a factor? Consider how children's growth in influenced both inside and outside the house.

5. The themes of community empowerment start to become apparent in both the new recruits that show up, drawn to Gus's magics, but also in the stadium filled with strangers who have never even encountered Gus, but heard about xer's troubles. Why do you think this was important for Gus?

6. Gender identity is the biggest theme of book 2. We learn through Gustopher's memories that gender has been a fluid concept, then a more rigid one. We begin looking through the lens at gender from not only a very old being, but one who is not human. How did this affect you? Has it changed how you see gender now?

Cranberry Orange Scones

Prep Time: 30 minutes -- Cook Time: 25 minutes
Total Time: 1 hour -- Yield: 8 large or 16 small scones

Ingredients

2 cups (250g) all-purpose flour (spooned & leveled), plus more for hands and work surface
½ cup (100g) granulated sugar
2 and ½ teaspoons baking powder
½ teaspoon salt
2 teaspoons orange zest (about 1 orange)
½ cup (8 Tbsp; 113g) unsalted butter, frozen
½ cup (120ml) heavy cream
1 large egg
1 teaspoon pure vanilla extract
1 heaping cup (125g) frozen cranberries
Optional: 1 Tablespoon (15ml) heavy cream and coarse sugar
1 cup (120g) confectioners' sugar
3 Tablespoons (30-45ml) orange juice

Instructions

1. Whisk flour, sugar, baking powder, salt, and orange zest together in a large bowl. Grate the frozen butter using a box grater. Add it to the flour mixture and combine with a pastry cutter, two forks, or your fingers until the mixture comes together in pea-sized

crumbs. Place in the refrigerator or freezer as you mix the wet ingredients together.

2. Whisk 1/2 cup heavy cream, the egg, and vanilla extract together in a small bowl. Drizzle over the flour mixture, add the cranberries, then mix together until everything appears moistened.

3. Pour onto the counter and, with floured hands, work dough into a ball as best you can. Dough will be sticky. If it's too sticky, add a little more flour. If it seems too dry, add 1-2 more Tablespoons heavy cream. Press into an 8-inch disc and, with a sharp knife or bench scraper, cut into 8 wedges.

4. Brush scones with remaining heavy cream and for extra crunch, sprinkle with coarse sugar. (You can do this before or after refrigerating in the next step.)

5. Place scones on a plate or lined baking sheet (if your fridge has space!) and refrigerate for at least 15 minutes.

6. Meanwhile, preheat oven to 400°F (204°C).

7. Line a large baking sheet with parchment paper or silicone baking mat. After refrigerating, arrange scones 2-3 inches apart on the prepared baking sheet(s).

8. Bake for 22-25 minutes or until golden brown around the edges and lightly browned on top. Remove from the oven and allow to cool for a few minutes as you make the glaze.

HOT TIP

To obtain a flaky center and a crumbly exterior, scone dough must remain cold. Cold dough won't over-spread either. Therefore, I highly recommend you chill the shaped scones for at least 15 minutes prior to baking. You can even refrigerate overnight for a quick breakfast in the morning.

Make the glaze

1. Whisk the confectioners' sugar and orange juice together. Add a little more confectioners' sugar to thicken or more juice to thin. Drizzle over scones.

2. Leftover iced or un-glazed scones keep well at room temperature for 2 days or in the refrigerator for 5 days.

https://sallysbakingaddiction.com/glazed-cranberry-orange-scones/#tasty-recipes-71017

Cranberry Rosemary Cookies

YIELDS: 30 PREP TIME: 15 mins TOTAL TIME: 55 mins

Ingredients

4 oz. fresh or frozen cranberries (about ¾ c.)
¼ c. Truvia Sweet Complete Granulated All-Purpose Sweetener
⅓ c. water
Pinch kosher salt
¼ tsp. orange zest
¾ c. (1 ½ sticks) butter, melted
1 tbsp. chopped fresh rosemary
½ c. Truvia Sweet Complete Granulated All-Purpose Sweetener
1 large egg
1 tsp. pure vanilla extract
½ tsp. kosher salt
1 ¾ c. all-purpose flour
¾ tsp. baking powder

Instructions

1. **Make cranberry jam**: In a small pot over medium heat, combine cranberries, sweetener, water, salt, and orange zest. Bring to a simmer and cook, stirring occasionally, until berries have burst and sauce is shiny and thickened, 8 to 10 minutes. Remove from heat and use a wooden spoon to stir and crush cranberries until mixture is mostly smooth. Let cool.

2. Preheat oven to 350° and line two baking sheets with parchment.

3. **Make cookie dough**: In a large bowl, whisk together melted butter, rosemary, and sweetener until smooth. Add egg, vanilla, and salt and stir to combine. Add flour and baking powder and fold until evenly combined.

4. Using a small cookie scoop or a large spoon, scoop 1" balls onto prepared baking sheets spaced 2" apart. Press a thumbprint into the center of each ball, 1/2" deep. Fill with a scant teaspoon of jam.

5. Bake until the bottoms of the cookies are golden, 13 to 14 minutes.

6. Cool on baking sheets before serving.

https://www.delish.com/cooking/recipe-ideas/a37416086/cranberry-thumbprint-cookies-recipe/

Horchaita

Measurements:

2 cups of water
1 cup brown or white rice
2 cups oat milk
2 cups Turbinado cane sugar
2 cinnamon sticks
6 cardamoms
3 cloves
Pinch of fennel seeds
3 peppercorns
3 tablespoons of ceylon BOPF black tea

Instructions

We made every attempt to find the instructions for this in Kevin Wilson's Chai Recipe book, in the captions of his videos, and online, but unfortunately, all we could find was this social media video. However, it's too delicious to not include, so we humbly beg your pardon for the lack of clear instruction.

https://www.instagram.com/p/CtPaBiCL-7o/

Chocolate Pomegranate Cookies

Prep Time: 20 minutes -- Cook Time: 25 minutes
Total Time: 40 minutes -- Servings: 22 cookies

Chocolate Cookies

- 1 box chocolate fudge cake mix {15.25 ounces}
- 2 large eggs
- ⅓ cup vegetable oil

Truffle Filling

- 1 ¼ cups milk chocolate chips
- ⅓ cup heavy cream

Topping

- ¼ cup pomegranate seeds

Instructions

Chocolate Cookies

Preheat the oven to 350°.

Combine the cake mix, eggs and vegetable oil in a medium bowl. Mix using a hand-held mixer {or by hand} until everything is totally combined and you have a thick and slightly sticky dough.

Use a medium cookie scoop or spoon and scoop mounds of dough into your hand. If the dough is too sticky, flour your hands and roll the dough into a smooth ball. Place the cookie dough mounds onto a silicone mat {or parchment} lined baking sheet.

Bake for 9-11 minutes. Remove from the oven and make an indentation in the middle of each cookie using your thumb or a tart shaper. Allow the cookies to cool on the baking sheet.

Truffle Filling

Once the cookies are cool combine the milk chocolate chips and heavy cream in a microwave-safe bowl and microwave for 30 seconds. Whisk the ingredients until everything is melted and shiny {if you need more time, add 10-second increments}.

Assembly

Use a small cookie scoop or spoon to fill each indentation with truffle filling and top with 5-6 pomegranate seeds while the filling is still wet.

Notes

- While the recipe calls for chocolate fudge cake mix, you can experiment with other cake mix flavors for variety.

- Do not over-bake the cookies. Bake the chocolate cake mix cookies until they are set up but not hard in the middle {it can be a bit hard to tell because you can't tell if chocolate cookies are turning golden brown}. Once you remove the cookies from the oven, allow them to cool completely on the baking sheet. The residual heat from the baking sheet will give you a perfect chewy cookie.

- Make the indentation in the middle of each cookie right after you remove them from the oven. I love to use a tart shaper but the end of a wooden spoon or your thumb works too.

- Add a heaping teaspoon of orange zest to the filling. This will add another great flavor that pairs perfectly with tart pomegranate.

- Store leftovers in an airtight container at room temperature or in the refrigerator for up to 3 days.

https://practicallyhomemade.com/easy-pomegranate-cookies/#recipe

Cinnamon Shortbread Cookies

Prep — 40 min (includes chilling) Cook — 22 min
Total — 1 hr 2 min — Makes 16 to 20 cookies

Ingredients

COOKIES

3 sticks (¾ pound) unsalted butter, at room temperature
1 cup granulated sugar
1 teaspoon vanilla extract
3½ cups all-purpose flour
2 teaspoons ground cinnamon
Kosher salt

SUGAR COATING

½ cup granulated sugar
½ teaspoon ground cinnamon
½ teaspoon ground nutmeg
¼ teaspoon ground cloves

Instructions

1. Preheat the oven to 350°F. Line two baking sheets with parchment paper.

2. **MAKE THE COOKIES:** In the bowl of an electric mixer fitted with the paddle attachment, mix the butter, the 1 cup sugar, vanilla and 1 tablespoon warm water on low speed until

they are just combined (don't whip it!). In a medium bowl, sift together the flour, the 2 teaspoons cinnamon and 1 teaspoon salt.

3. With the mixer still on low, slowly add the flour mixture to the butter mixture, mixing just until the dough comes together in large clumps. Transfer to a floured surface and shape into a flat disk. Wrap in plastic wrap and chill for just 30 minutes.

4. On a floured cutting board, roll the dough ½ inch thick and cut with a large (3½-inch) star cutter (or any other shape you like). Place the cookies one inch apart on the prepared baking sheets and bake until the edges just begin to brown, 20 to 22 minutes.

5. **MAKE THE SUGAR COATING:** Meanwhile, combine the ½ cup sugar, cinnamon, nutmeg and cloves in a medium bowl. As soon as the cookies come out of the oven, sprinkle them thickly with the sugar mixture and cool on the baking sheets. When the cookies are cool, shake off the excess sugar mixture and serve warm or at room temperature.

NOTE: To make the cookies ahead, prepare the dough and cut out the cookies, then refrigerate or freeze in containers. Bake and sprinkle with the sugar mixture before serving. Wrap the baked cookies and store at room temperature for several days.

https://www.purewow.com/recipes/ina-garten-cinnamon-spiced-shortbread

Ginger Peach Soda

YIELDS: 8   PREP TIME: 15 mins
TOTAL TIME: 45 mins

Ingredients

1 c. sugar
2 tbsp. minced fresh ginger
2 very ripe peaches, (about 2 /3 pound), halved, pitted, and thinly sliced
2 liters seltzer, chilled
16 fresh mint leaves, for garnish

Instructions

1. In a medium saucepan over medium-low heat, bring 1 cup water, sugar, and ginger to a gentle simmer, stirring to dissolve sugar. Remove simple syrup from heat, cover, and steep for about 30 minutes.

2. Over a medium bowl, pour syrup through a fine-mesh sieve, pressing minced ginger against sieve with the back of a spoon to extract flavor. Discard ginger. Cover bowl with plastic wrap, and refrigerate until well chilled.

3. Evenly distribute peach slices among 8 tall glasses. For each glass, lightly press peaches with the back of a wooden spoon to release their juice. Pour about 2 tablespoons chilled syrup over peaches. (Store remaining syrup in refrigerator for up to 2 weeks.) Add ice cubes; then top with seltzer. Stir to distribute syrup,

peach juice, and seltzer evenly. Garnish with 2 mint leaves.

https://www.womansday.com/food-recipes/food-drinks/recipes/a39503/ginger-peach-soda-recipe-clv0613/

Book 3 Sneak Peek

An exclusive look into the final book of The Gus Chronicles

1958, Certaldo, Tuscany, Italy

The summer sun beat down on her back as 16-year-old Marguerita stood in front of a pile of old masonry figures bleached white from years in the sun. There wasn't much to do in her small town, so when there was an event, you went, even if you didn't know, or cared, what the event was.

Marguerita scowled as she took in the broken statues around her. She was usually scowling. Her mother was always telling her, "Chi non ha testa abbia buone gambe," which basically meant, in Marguerita's case, that if she was going to be a difficult personality, she had better be prepared to excel in other ways. Marguerita didn't believe in pretending to be happy, in pleasing others, or in telling white lies to satisfy egos. This had made her deeply unpopular most of her childhood.

The masonry had come from an old stonecarver's house after he had passed away. His children had already found a use for the house, the grounds, and the furniture. But the masonry blocks and statues weren't selling at the markets, and the family wanted to liquidate the heavy items as soon as possible. The church elders arranged a rummage sale to raise money to repair the bell tower. The church had been "raising money for the bell tower" for over 100 years, and everyone knew it really went to pay for the trips to the hair salon of the priest's wife, but no one cared enough to kick up a fuss.

Marguerita didn't care about masonry either, as she had been surrounded her whole life in this small, suffocating Catholic town by beautiful items in every direction.

There were angel reliefs and marble cemetery blocks, geometric-patterned bricks, waist-high columns, tiles of every color, shape and size. There was even a gargoyle statue, its eyes half-closed in sleepy contentment.

Marguerita wandered for a while, touching the different textures and ignoring the other village members around her. She was considered the strange one in town, the one who didn't behave politely, and she didn't get along with the other teenagers. She was "too smart, too full of herself." Girls her age should "wear dresses, style their hair to catch a man, be modest and not speak their minds." Marguerita couldn't be further from all those things. She learned how to sew clothes just so she could wear trousers. She stared at people on purpose, just to make them uncomfortable until they looked away. She read voraciously, and therefore, had many opinions. She did take some time on her hair, but that was for her own benefit, as the long, tawny locks would often tangle and catch on things if she didn't take a few minutes to tie it back with a scarf or, if desperate, a piece of rope.

She drifted back to examine the gargoyle again. She felt drawn to the little outcast who had ended up here. How had a gargoyle come to Certaldo, anyway? It's not as if the village could afford the fancy decorations of the larger churches. And gargoyles usually came in pairs. Was there another one nearby? Marguerita searched and searched, and could only find the one. She tried to ask the man running the rummage sale, but he waved away her questions with impatience. She was getting tired from the heat, so on impulse, she lifted the statue in the air from the back of the expansive yard, huffed and puffed all the way to the front, cutting in the line that had formed there, and thunked it on the wooden table to pay. She dug in her pocket for the change she'd been saving up for months. She tossed the lira down, and the man shouted at her as the wind picked up, lifting the bills in the air. She laughed as she hoisted the statue into her bicycle basket, the man yelling at her while chasing the bills in circles as the wind danced them just out of reach.

Back at her house, her mother only waved from the kitchen as the back door banged. Marguerita stomped awkwardly up the stairs to her attic bedroom. The heat was oppressive up here before the sun went down, but at least she would have her favorite thing: privacy.

"I am going to leave this place one day, *bambino assonnato*," she said. "Little sleepy one, that suits you for now. Until we find your name. Do you want to come with me, eh? Do you want to come with me to see the world?"

She studied the gargoyle closer, noting a few dents in the material. It looked like someone had taken a gun and shot at the statue, probably for target practice.

"You poor thing! Who would want to hurt a sweet little pearl like you?" she cooed, pulling out her mandolin and strumming a few chords tunelessly. It was one of the reasons she wasn't a target for bullies; she was a gifted musician and the village loved her playing.

Her father had given her the mandolin as a birthday gift when she turned 12, and she took to it instantly. It was one of the first things that felt natural to her, something that felt like home. Next to books, of course.

Marguerita sighed. She knew her mother would expect her to come down and help make dinner, so she tucked her mandolin carefully back in its case, patted the gargoyle statue on the head, and went down to make dinner.

The evening passed uneventfully, though Marguerita did take a nice walk down the road after dinner to see the full moon. She went to bed, snuffing out the candle as she drifted off, watching the moonlight bathe the gargoyle in a bluish glow.

Sometime in the middle of the night, Marguerita awoke suddenly. She felt something was watching her. She yelped as she saw that in place of the gargoyle, a dragon — *a live dragon* — had come to life, and was staring at her with glowing eyes, one silver eye and one green. As she stared in shock, she heard a voice in her head, somehow both foreign and yet very gentle.

"Yes, I will come with you."

OTHER OFFERINGS

Other Offerings by Promise Press

<u>Cozy Adventure series:</u>
Guarding Gus-Book 1

<u>Romance/Autobiographical fiction:</u>
Stockings Required, Tales of a Cigarette & Candy Girl

<u>The Spicy Coloring Book series:</u>
Stabby Feelings: a Humorous Floral Swearing Coloring Book
for Adult Stress Relief
Fucking Brilliant: An Empowerment Coloring Book
How Dare You: A Humorous, Scandalous Coloring Book

<u>Halloween coloring books:</u>
Perky Goth Halloween Coloring Book: Vol 1 & 2

<u>Self-Help:</u>
Intention Coloring: Color Your Goals into Reality

Go to www.promisepress.org for even more items!

www.ingramcontent.com/pod-product-compliance
Lightning Source LLC
Chambersburg PA
CBHW070505300726
48975CB00007B/2327